BEHIND *the* Cascades

T.J. DEAL

Word Candy
PUBLISHING

To the audacious and badass women who summoned the strength to not only change their zip code but to forge their own path and create their own destiny.

Prologue

Charlie

Six years prior—

The grass is already dewy and wet against my bare legs as I stare out at my favorite pond. It belongs to my godmother, Connie, and her late husband, Roger.

I've spent my entire life chasing my older brother and his friends out here—our friends, really. We've had countless barbecues, birthday parties, and late-night bonfires by this pond. It normally holds memories of laughter and joy, but today is different. Today, it's filled with only memories of sadness and loss.

The sun set what felt like hours ago; the only light is from the full moon's reflection off the pond. Lightning bugs flew around for a while, hypnotizing me into a rhythmic lullaby, but they've since stopped. I have no idea what time it is, only that it must be the middle of the night.

At some point, someone draped an old quilt over my shoulders to keep the evening chill at bay. I don't know who it was or if they're still here, but I don't really care.

I haven't moved from this spot since I fell here hours ago. I ran out here by myself to get away from everyone and everything falling apart around me.

Last night, my parents left to pick up dinner for us and never returned. A driver swerved into their lane, hitting them head on. The man who decided to have a few too many and then drove took them from us in an instant. Killing them and himself in the process. They won't get to see my brother, Drew, graduate from high school next year. My mom won't help me get ready for my senior prom, and my dad won't get to walk me down the aisle for my wedding.

Drew is angry. So, so angry. Storming around the house on a warpath of self destruction.

Connie hasn't stopped crying since yesterday—big, loud sobs that threaten to drown me.

Hayes, Connie's son and Drew's best friend, constantly assessed the three of us, like we are about to break. He bounced between us, trying to offer comfort and support, but his efforts only seemed futile.

Our lives had once again changed forever. It was the same when Roger first got diagnosed with cancer and then passed away only a few short weeks later.

I couldn't take it anymore—feeling all of their emotions while trying to deal with my own. So here I sit, alone. Avoiding the anger, the sadness, and the worry.

"Sunshine." A low timber voice breaks through my thoughts. *Maybe not alone.*

Of course, it's Hayes here. He's called me Sunshine for as long as I can remember. The worrier of our group of five. The protector. The one who makes sure everyone else is okay, even when he's not okay himself. The one I've been in love with since I knew what a "crush" was.

I glance toward where his voice came from. He's sitting on

the grass a couple feet away from me, shivering. I hadn't even known he was there.

"Come here, you idiot." I extend my arm out so that he can get under the blanket.

"Rude, considering I'm the one that brought that blanket." He doesn't move from his spot, though. His beautiful brown eyes searched my face, trying to read my emotions.

All that I can see is the pain and exhaustion etched in his young features, and it feels like my heart is breaking even more.

"Please, just come here," I plead, my voice filled with concern. He finally relents, slowly inching closer until he tucked his large frame beside me under the blanket.

The signature smell of peppermint mints enveloped me, and I snuggled in closer to his side. He's carried around his dad's antique tin of mints since he passed away a few years ago. Uncle Roger called it his good-luck tin, saying he made it home every deployment because he had it with him. He'd buy the same brand of mints, refill his tin, and toss the new box into the garbage like it had insulted him.

"What do I do without them?" I asked him softly, barely maintaining my composure.

He doesn't respond immediately, his gaze fixed on the pond.

After a moment, he takes a deep breath and leans his cheek against the top of my head. "I don't know," he admits, his voice filled with uncertainty. "But we'll figure it out together."

Chapter One

Charlie

Wednesday, September 28.

"Dess, they're going to freak out when they see us here. I can't believe you talked me into this." I say as I rub my temples in a circular motion, leaning against the check-in counter of the hotel. It's late, we just took a last-minute flight, and I worked all day.

Odessa, my best friend of nearly ten years, insisted we fly to Las Vegas to surprise the guys for Hayes 24th birthday. My brother, Drew, and Hayes have been friends since before I was born. They became friends with Everett, Odessa's brother, when they were in middle school. Ev always brought Dess with him wherever he went, and Drew and Hayes were mandated to bring me. Odessa and I joke that we were destined to be friends but really we didn't have any other choice. Our overprotective older brothers wouldn't let anyone else around us.

She gives me a devilish smirk, throwing her long blonde hair over her shoulder. "Good. Those jerks should have invited us. The fact they didn't is reason enough to give them a verbal smackdown. In person. Possibly with fists." Her nonchalant shrug at the end implies that she's only half serious, but I can see the mischievous glint in her eyes. Knowing Dess, she would have no problem following through with it. The woman packs a mean left punch, and each of the guys has received a few dead arms at her expense.

The guys hadn't even told us they were planning this trip so they have no idea that we arrived the night before them. Connie, Hayes mom, and the one who practically raised me after my parents died, mentioned that all three guys would be together for the first time in years. In Vegas. Without us. Surrounded by booze, gambling, and who knows what else. A few years ago, they invited—more like drug— us along to every-thing they went to. The five of us were a package deal, but since they graduated high school and moved away, everything's changed.

Drew and Hayes joined the Navy, went through bootcamp, and then went right into BUD/S. Both of them officially became Navy SEALs a few years ago. *And have egos to match.* Drew rarely texts and only calls for holidays. Hayes keeps in touch more regularly, a lot through social media but I think we talk at least once a week. That's why it was so surprising when Connie mentioned his birthday in Vegas. He hadn't said a word to me about them going. I'm doing my best to pretend that didn't hurt, but the sting of rejection is always present with Hayes. Especially since my "crush" is still very much alive and well, six years later. It's not my fault the man is aging like fine wine. With each deployment, he comes back a little gruffer, a little more muscular, and a lot sexier. Not that I've noticed. We are friends. Only friends. *So I keep telling myself.*

Everett decided to join the army, going from high school to flight school, and has been crushing it as a Rotary Wing Avia-tor. He flies all over the world, constantly being deployed, and rarely keeps in touch. I honestly can't remember the last time we talked—maybe my birthday? For the obligatory "happy birthday" text. Odessa typically keeps me filled in on his life though and I'm sure vice versa.

When I told Odessa about the guys trip, she immediately bought us plane tickets and booked a hotel room. The woman is nothing if not efficient and has the paychecks to back it. She had everything booked before I even agreed to the trip. Which is probably a good thing because I absolutely would have backed out. For starters, I'm not twenty-one and will be using a fake ID that my coworker Ava lent me. She's only a few years older than me, but we are roughly the same height and have the same eye color. I've used it before and bouncers don't even bat an eye at the photo. Second, the guys clearly don't want us there or else they would've invited us. Thirdly, I'm a complete scaredy-cat when it comes to Hayes and telling him my feelings. Seeing him flirt and dance with other women may damn well kill me.

I groan when I see the clock in our hotel room after we finally check in. It's just after eleven here, but it would be after two a.m. back in South Carolina. I also had class this morning and then worked a full-day at the office. Technically, I should only be part-time until I graduate next spring, but I tend to put in full-time hours to help Ava. The hours are dauntless, but I love the fast-paced office. I'm Ava's assistant and she's the assistant of billionaire Noah Ledger. Noah's only in the office half the time and the rest he's traveling around the world, making lucrative business deals and investing in commercial real estate. That leaves me and Ava to handle everything while he's gone. Well, Ava handles most of it and delegates the easy stuff to me.

Thankfully, she had no problem with me leaving at the last minute; if anything, she demanded it. I walked into work and she handed me a suitcase with some of her designer dresses, her ID, and condoms. Her exact words were, "Make that man *your* man, or I will." *Like that'll ever happen.*

"**W**akey-wakey, Char!" Odessa hollers from the other side of our hotel room. My brain refuses to open my eyes to the bright room. I feel hungover and I didn't even drink last night. The anxiety of seeing Hayes had me tossing and turning all night, despite the plush bedding.

I quickly yank my blankets up and throw my pillow over my head when I hear the distinct noise of a cart rolling into our room. Odessa must have ordered room-service and I'm in no state for an attendant to see me right now.

Light conversation filters between Odessa and the person dropping off our breakfast. She is the queen of small talk and flirtation so I have no doubt the unsuspecting male room-service attendant is already under her spell. He chuckles at whatever she says and then, thankfully, leaves.

She yanks the pillow off my head and my eyes fly open. "Charlotte Amelia Reynolds, get your ass out of bed. You have exactly one hour until the guys land." *Shit.*

I grab my phone off the nightstand and grumble when I see that she isn't just messing with me. It's already well into the morning and Connie has been keeping us in the loop about their plans. Her birthday present to Hayes was this hotel suite so she knew exactly which hotel and even which room they'd be in. She booked the Skyloft for us all and then made sure to let the front desk know they couldn't inform the guys that we were up here. Luckily, it has four rooms, so only two people have to share. With any luck, I'll be sharing with Hayes.

"Coffee, shower, food." Odessa sternly points me in the

direction of all the things I need to do. Only half-begrudgingly, I go. I've been excited to take advantage of the double-headed waterfall shower since last night. Everything about the suite is dripping in luxury. Not that I should be surprised; Connie chose it and she always goes above and beyond. Especially when it comes to fancy things.

Forty-five minutes later, I feel human again. I'm convinced iced coffee and a hot shower are the ultimate cure for almost all of life's problems.

Dess lets out a low whistle when I finally emerge from the bathroom. "Damn, girl. If Hayes doesn't man up, I guarantee there will be ten other guys lining up to do the job."

I smirk back and try to laugh off what she said, but deep down, I know she's right. I've been pining after a guy for years who barely notices my presence. Sure, I've gone on dates. A lot of dates, actually. But when you compare every guy to Hayes, they all fall short. He's kind, funny, and sexy as hell. The trifecta. The complete package. Throw on the compliments he showers me with and I'm gone. Hook, line, and sinker. It's no wonder I haven't been able to get over him. Every time I try, he reels me back in with a "thinking of you" text. Bleh. I'm weak. I know I'm weak. Yet, here I am. A skimpy bikini, hair curled, and face full of makeup to lounge by the pool.

"I'm willing to admit, I look good. It's his loss if he doesn't notice."

Her evil chuckle has me feeling nervous. "Oh, he's going to notice. It's only a matter of whether he pulls his head out of his ass and does something about it."

Chapter Two

Hayes

The hotel my mom booked for us is way out of our normal budget. Hell, it's out of 75 percent of the population's budget. She doesn't throw her money around often, but I know my grandparents left her a healthy trust fund. The one they left me is only a fraction of hers, and it's enough to cover any modest person's expenses for the rest of their lives. I haven't touched it yet, but someday I plan on leaving the Navy and settling down. Buying a house with some property and living a low-key life. As of right now, that future is looking pretty lonely. Especially considering the only woman I've ever been in love with is so off-limits I won't even let myself dream about it.

"I'm Face-Timing mom the second we get in our room. This place is insane!" Drew has called my mom "mom" for years, even before she moved him and Charlie into our house after they lost their parents.

Once we reach our floor, we have to use our keycard to get off the elevator. The cart doors open to an expansive hallway with only a few doors. It's not the most exclusive floor, but damn close.

I gesture to the door that is ours and Drew scans the key card. We all freeze the second the door starts to open and we hear giggles on the other side.

"What the—?" Everett begins to question the sound but is interrupted by Odessa's unmistakable voice on the other end.

"Hurry up, losers!"

Drew shoves the door open the rest of the way while I'm still too stunned to move.

Right on the other side, leaning up against the back of a couch and looking directly at us, are Odessa and Charlie. My Charlie. My so-off-limits it isn't even funny, Charlie. My Sunshine.

Everything about her looks as good as I remember. She's always been gorgeous, but every year, I swear, she gets more beautiful. My own personal torture is looking at her and knowing I can't have her. Before, it was just the age difference. A three year difference might not be much but when you've grown up with someone, it felt like ten. Add on that she was my best friend's little sister *and* we lived together because her parents had just died... Well, that alone felt like enough to keep me away. Now, though, it's all of that, along with knowing that I could never truly deserve her. Not after all the things I've seen and done. Charlie is pure and good, and I'm, well, I'm the opposite. I'm not evil, but I'm the one they call to take care of the evil. And if that doesn't leave some eternal marks on your soul, I don't know what will.

She nibbles on the corner of her nail, clearly nervous for our reaction to them crashing our party. Only she isn't crashing. If I had thought she could be here, I would have flown her out in a second. I hadn't wanted to ask because I know how busy she is with classes and work. *And because I didn't want to walk around with a hard-on all weekend.*

"Holy shit. I'm gonna have a B.F.!" Everett waves his arms

around, expecting everyone to get the reference. He's quoted movies for longer than I can remember but usually the only person that gets them is...

"Shut up. You're not going to have a bitch fit." Odessa rolls her eyes but laughs and hugs her brother. The two of them have always looked like twins, despite the two year age difference. Blonde hair, blue eyes, and both over six feet tall.

Ignoring them, I step around, my eyes focused on Charlie. My hand instantly goes to the tin in my pocket, tapping it to calm my nerves. If I hadn't just popped a mint into my mouth on the elevator, I'd be chomping on three of them. A nervous habit I picked up after my dad died. Inhaling mints as if the coolness will calm my inner anxiety.

Drew was the first to give her a hug, but he laughed lovingly at her apology for showing up. "You kidding? The five of us are going to rage like old times!"

She chuckles back but I see the nerves still playing behind those emerald eyes when she looks at me.

"Happy birthday, Hayes!" She saunters over and I swear she throws an extra sway in her hips just to drive me crazy.

"Thanks, Sunshine." I pull her into me and whisper it low into her ear, even though everyone already knows I call her Sunshine. They think it's because of the color of her hair, it's always been just a shade more red than blonde. However, the real reason is that every room she walks into, she lights up. Anytime I was having a bad day or in a bad mood, she knew exactly what to say and how to make me laugh. Still does.

She leans away, but at least now she has a small smile. "Is it okay that we are invading your birthday party?"

"Yes! I wanted to—"

Odessa chooses that moment to interrupt us, throwing her arm around my shoulder and grinning. "Hayes! The big two-four! You ready to party like it's 1999?" She winks, causing me to shake my head in amusement.

"Nope, but I'm ready to get down to that pool and chill." The girls are already wearing their swimsuits and cover-ups, and pool bags are waiting by their feet. I must be a masochist because I'm already desperate to see Charlie in the bikini she is hiding. Five minutes in and this is turning out to be the best birthday I've ever had. A swanky hotel, my closest friends, and a pool bar calling my name.

I spoke too soon. Worst fucking birthday ever. The pool bar that was once calling my name now feels like a battleground for Charlie's attention. Attention that I crave but know I shouldn't have.

She parades herself around the pool in that tiny bikini, showing off a body that I can't touch. Which wouldn't be as big of a problem if every man didn't ogle her as she walked by. It takes more self-control than I'd like to not stab the eyes out of their heads with the tiny plastic cocktail sword from my drink. Between her and Odessa, our cabana has felt like a zoo attraction. Men walk by and stare a little too hard, trying to get their attention. Drew and Everett look as pissed as I feel, but for very different reasons.

I lay back on the cabana, closing my eyes so that I don't murder one of these innocent bystanders for merely looking at my girl who isn't even my girl. My breathing just starts to even out when I feel the edge of the bed dip as someone climbs onto the lounger next to me. I don't have to peek my eyes open to know that it's her. My body feels on fire everywhere she touches me, always has. Charlie's never outright said she has feelings for me, but the signs are there. *Or maybe I just read into them too much.* The touching, the blatant nerves around only me, the blush I saw hit her cheeks when I caught her watching me take my shirt off.

On one hand, I love it. Love her body pressed up against me. Want to mark her like she's mine. Let every asshole around here know they can't have her. On the other hand, she's too close and I don't trust myself to not break. Years of resolve crumbling down because of one bikini. One very sexy and distracting bikini. The temptation to reach out and touch her is relentless, but I know I need to keep my distance to avoid crossing any lines.

I take a deep breath and try to keep my eyes closed. My senses are on overdrive. Between the drinks and her presence, I'm quickly losing control.

"How's your birthday so far?" She bumps her bare shoulder into mine and I can feel the heat radiating off her skin.

I open my eyes and force a smile, trying to push away the thoughts that threaten to consume me. "It's good. Glad you two came. Wouldn't have been the same without you."

She nods but doesn't say anything. I follow her gaze to see Everett, Odessa, and Drew laughing while sitting by the bar.

"I didn't get to finish what I was saying earlier. I really did want to invite you. You and Odessa. But you've barely had any time to blink in the last few months. You're so busy with work and school. I didn't want you to feel obligated." All of that is true, but I don't add in that the main reason is that I was afraid too. Being around her always sends me into a tailspin. My conscience in a never ending battle with my desire.

"Never obligated when it comes to you. Next time, I want the invite." The grin she sends me makes my heart skip a beat.

"Yeah? I'll remember that."

We're both quiet for a few minutes, soaking up the moment. I keep my fingers threaded together behind my head. I don't trust myself not to wrap my arm around her shoulders and bring her closer to me.

"Any plans after graduation?" I ask, trying to ease the tension building inside me.

Her delicate fingers begin playing with the end of her long braid. "Was thinking about taking a year off and traveling. Getting out of South Carolina."

"Alone? Or following Odessa around the world?" I ask with a little too much worry in my voice. Odessa moved to New York after she graduated high school. She had already been doing some modeling, but her career took off when she got up there. She's now one of the top high fashion models, and travels all the time. I don't know which would be worse, her wandering around the US by herself or her and Odessa in another country. The two of them have always been trouble together.

She lets out a soft chuckle at my overreaction. "Alone. But, maybe around the world? I don't know. You four live such exciting lives! I want to experience some new things."

"No," I scoff back.

Her eyes widen when she looks at me. "No?"

"Sorry, *hell* no. You aren't gallivanting around the world by yourself."

"Hayes, I wasn't asking. You have no—"

I cut her off before she could start her argument. "Sunshine... I know that I don't have a right to say what you can and can't do. But if you think I'd ever allow you to put yourself in danger, you're wrong."

"That's not fair. Odessa—"

"Odessa has bodyguards! She has an entire team following her around, keeping her safe."

Her eyes narrow to almost slits while she glares at me. "Stop interrupting me. I'm not five. I'm not the teenager I was when you left. Believe it or not, I'm capable of making my own decisions."

"Oh, trust me. I know." I rake my gaze up her body and arch my eyebrow when I reach her eyes.

Both of us stay silent for a few breaths. I can tell she wants to go off on me but is holding back.

I reach out and grab her right hand with my left, lacing our fingers together. "Please trust me on this. We see things all the time. Classified things. Things that happen in 'safe' countries. Things that will never make the news because of how truly sick and twisted they are. If Odessa didn't have a team with her, I'd say the same thing to her." A team that Drew and I carefully handpicked, vetted, and trained. Neither of the girls has any idea of the things that go down all over the world. Hell, I only know a fraction and it's still enough to make me question every-thing I thought I knew about humanity.

Her eyes search mine, looking for any insincerity. She squeezes my hand once and then one side of her mouth begins to turn up. "Okay, I won't go alone. But you owe me a trip to Europe."

Relief floods through me at her agreement. "I'll take you anywhere you want, beautiful."

My flirty banter causes her lips to part as she inhales a tiny gasp. She glances from my eyes down to my lips and back up again. Our lips are only a few inches away at this point, a light gust of wind and they'd be touching.

"Hey, lovebirds!" Odessa shouts, ruining our moment once again.

Charlie drops my hand like it burned her and then scoots away from me. I know I should be thankful that we were inter-rupted, but all I feel is irritated.

"Y'all ready to head up and get ready for dinner?" Drew

asks, his southern accent sounding a little thicker since he's been drinking.

I chuckle and stand up to start packing our stuff. "Yep. I could use a shower."

Odessa mumbles something under her breath that sounds a lot like "a cold one," but I choose to ignore the jest. She's always in everyone's business and ever since I confessed my feelings toward Charlie a few years ago, she has had no problem fucking with me. In my defense, I was drunk on Thanksgiving and Charlie had brought a date. Dess called me out the moment dinner was over and she caught me alone. Not once has Drew or Everett given me shit or attempted to kick my ass though so I know she hasn't told my secret.

Chapter Three

Hayes

Lounging back on the couch, I kick my feet up on the coffee table. The cold beer in my hand does nothing to calm my edginess from earlier. The girls escaped to their bathroom to get ready for dinner tonight and we haven't seen them since. I'm itching to drag Charlie out of there just to be near here, but I know that would be counterintuitive. Distance is better, safer.

Drew plops himself down in the armchair across from me, taking up more space than I thought possible. He's not that much bigger than I am—a few inches in height—but sitting in that chair makes him look like a giant trying to fit into a toddler's chair.

"You comfortable? Looks like your big ass is going to break that chair."

He chuckles back. "I'll just tell mom it was you when it snaps."

Everett sits off to the side at the kitchen counter, snacking on food from the large birthday basket my mom ordered. "Happy to go along with that story!"

"The fuck? It's my birthday. Where's the love?"

"Speaking of love. What was with Odessa's 'lovebird' comment down at the pool?" Drew throws out the question like he's genuinely confused.

Guilt hits me as I nervously glance between him and a laughing Everett who says. "Don't act like you don't know!"

"Know what?" Drew looks at me, eyebrows raised.

"Shit. You naive SOB. Hayes has been in love with Char since what? Our senior year?"

"Fuck off, Everett." I grumble out. I don't want to see the hurt on Drew's face right now so I grab some mints and pop them into my mouth. Drew and I have been best friends since we were babies and we've always told each other everything. He's ranted for hours about any guy Charlie has ever talked to and how they aren't good enough for her. I'm not the exception here, I'm the rule. He hasn't just seen the worst of me; he's been there right alongside me through it all. He knows how fucked my head is because his is the same. There's no way he'll be okay with me having feelings for her.

"You love Charlie? Does she know?" I finally look up and see his shocked expression. At least he's not yelling at me or throwing a punch. *Yet.*

"She doesn't know."

"No fucking way, man. You pussy! Why haven't you told her?" Not at all the reaction I was expecting, but a small flicker of relief lights through my chest.

Everett's grinning like a cheshire cat from his stool. "He was too afraid you'd kick his ass."

I reach for the throw pillow and lob it at his head. He catches it and cackles his signature Everett cackle.

"She's young and she's your sister. She's always been off-limits."

Drew shakes his head and looks at me like I'm crazy. "You're the best guy I know. Why wouldn't I want my sister to be with you? There's no one in the world more loyal and protective than you. I just can't believe I didn't see it before! It all makes sense, though. You talk to her more than I do."

"After all the shit we've seen and done? We're still in it! We could be leaving soon, again. You want your sister wrapped up in that? Like our mom's were." I scoff, knowing I hit a sensitive subject. Our dad's met during the first phase of hell week and became best friends. They didn't get out of the Navy until Drew and I were in elementary school. Our mom's were saints, raising us alone while our dad's were always deployed or training.

"That's not for either of us to decide. Charlie is strong enough to make that decision by herself."

"She's too good for me." I shake my head; he's still not getting it. Even with his blessing, I won't drag her down into my darkness.

"She's too good for anyone! But there isn't a man out there that would treat her better than you would."

"I might." Everett shrugs and winks at me. I know he's fucking with me, trying to ease the tension but I still want to throttle him for the insinuation.

"See? You gonna let this *clown* who doesn't even get his hands dirty take your girl?" Everett flys Apaches into enemy territory and fires missiles without even breaking a sweat, but that doesn't mean we don't like to give him shit for going Army.

Everett's loud guffaw has me chuckling along with Drew. I know the point he's trying to prove, but I've put up too many barriers in my mind to fully accept what he's saying.

"What's so funny out here?" Odessa asks as she walks out of the hall. Charlie follows behind, the sight of her nearly taking my breath away. She curled her hair and left it loose, hanging behind her shoulders. The emerald dress she has on fits her like a glove and matches her eyes. The wedges she has on don't make her as tall as Odessa, but within an inch or two. She's a knockout and I'm the dumbass who is letting her slip through my fingers.

"Talking about Everett being a chump compared to us." Drew smirks.

I roll my eyes dramatically and shake my head at Odessa. She laughs and walks into the kitchen. "Anyone need a road beer? We should get going."

Drew and Everett both stand up and walk into the kitchen but Charlie remains awkwardly in the hall, not saying anything. She looks anywhere but at me, a fake smile plastered on her face.

"Sunshine." Her gaze snaps to mine and I raise my eyebrows. "You good?"

"Yep." Her tone sounds light, almost cheerful, but I know she's lying.

In three large steps, I've cleared the distance between us. I lightly touch her arm and watch as her shoulders fall slightly. "We either talk about it now or when we get back."

"Come on, y'all! We don't want to be late!" Odessa hollers from the doorway and for the third time today, I've detested her timing.

***

The steakhouse Everett found is anything but traditional, looking more like a speakeasy than a classic steakhouse. The jazz music playing softly in the background and the glowing chandeliers create a warm and intimate atmosphere. It'd be the perfect place for a first date with Charlie, but instead we have third-fourth-and-fifth wheels.

The hostess guides us through the restaurant to our table,

and I follow behind Charlie as closely as I can. She has me shooting daggers at any man that dares give her a second glance as she walks by. Most of them sheepishly look away when they notice me, but the few that dare hold my glare have me feeling murderous.

We all sit down at a circular booth and I make sure to plant myself right next to Charlie, sitting so close that our thighs touch. I'm heading down a dangerous road, but the way she's avoiding me has me on edge. The conversation I had with the guys early weighs heavily on my mind. Drew was right. I may not be good enough for her, but I can't think of anyone that is. She's the dream girl.

Odessa snaps me out of my thoughts. "What do you think, birthday boy? Club or gambling after this?"

I shrug noncommittally. "Who's sayin' that we can't do both? It's Vegas. The night is young, the drinks are going down easy, and the company is top-notch."

I wink at Charlie and the grin she blesses me with has me feeling at ease again.

"Is that?" Charlie gasps as she looks over my shoulder. I look just in time to see Heather, Drew's ex-girlfriend, walking toward our table.

"Yep." I reach down and lace my fingers through Charlies. She squeezes once, reassuringly. Heather and I have always butt heads. Never in front of Drew, but we've both made it clear that we aren't going to be friends. Since high school, the two of them have been a revolving door of breaking up and getting back together.

Drew hasn't noticed yet, laughing at something Everett said. I kick him under the table and nod toward the she-devil approaching our table.

His eyes widen slightly before he shakes his head and

smiles. He slides out of the booth to greet her. "Hey! What are you doing here?"

Maleficent grins mischievously, her eyes flickering around the table while she hugs him. "I'm in town for Laura's bachelorette party!" She gestures toward the table of scantily clad girls wearing sashes. They all look like they should be on a pole rather than having a nice dinner.

Charlie squeezes my hand a little harder and I resist the urge to chuckle. She's always had similar feelings about Heather as I have. Never outright hatred, but we both agree Heather cares about herself and only herself. And maybe her plastic surgeon.

"Chad finally proposed? Good for him."

"What has all of you in Vegas?" She doesn't glance at us again. I guarantee she'll only be focused on sinking those red talons back into Drew.

I hear Odessa's humorless laugh and look over to see her roll her eyes. Everett tries to scold her under his breath but it only spurs Dess on further. "What? They've been on-and-off for *years* and she doesn't even know it's his best friend's birthday."

My teeth hurt from clenching them so hard and trying not to chuckle. Odessa, the wildcard, has no filter, and I love her for it. She calls it like she sees it. Am I offended that Heather doesn't remember my birthday? Not in the slightest, but I appreciate Odessa's protectiveness.

Heather's smile falters just a touch but she recovers quickly. "Oh my god! I completely forgot. Happy birthday, Hayes! Where are y'all going after this? I'll buy you a shot."

I nod and offer a tight smile but don't respond. There's no way I'm revealing that information. If Drew wants her there, he can invite her.

"We were just talking about that. I'll text you when we set

plans." His grin widens as he hugs her again. "It's really good to see you."

Charlie's nails dig into my hand and I shake my head. That man only thinks with his dick when it comes to Heather and as much as I hate it, it's not our place to call him on it.

Thankfully, Heather walks away, her blonde ponytail swinging dramatically as she left. The mood of the table shifts to slightly uncomfortable. None of us know how to handle the Heather situation or our distaste for her.

Leave it to Everett to break the ice by starting to sing. "What do tigers dream of when they take a little tiger snooze?"

Odessa curses under her breath but grins. "Honestly surprised you last this long before making a 'Hangover' reference."

Charlie tries to pull her hand away but I keep it locked in mine until our food arrives. Apparently, Drew's approval changed everything. All I can think about is convincing Charlie to be mine. No better birthday gift than getting the girl of my dreams.

Chapter Four

Charlie

The club that Odessa dragged us to is loud, overcrowded, and smells like sweat and alcohol. Yet, there isn't anywhere else I'd rather be. Well, maybe in a hotel room with Hayes. Alone... But this is an okay second place. Hayes hasn't taken his eyes off of me since we got here. He's been different tonight—more attentive, more flirty, more touchy. Either the booze is flowing more freely than I thought, or he's letting his guard down.

The guys reserved a table for us, splurging on bottle service and making sure we had the nicest spot in the club. It was great until Drew invited Heather and her hoes. I mean, friends. They waltzed in half-naked and after spending ten minutes with them, I could feel my IQ dropping. Dess didn't last more than five minutes before quietly escaping to the dance floor without anyone but me noticing. I glared at her retreating back the entire time she walked away, but knew it was probably for the better. No reason for these women to ruin her night, not when she doesn't have a stake in the game.

Drew and Heather excused themselves to go dance as well.

She's been all over him since she got here, and my stupid brother hasn't stopped smiling. He thinks he's sly, but she's got him wrapped around her finger. I wouldn't be surprised if he ends up marrying her and then divorced within the first three years. The thought has me downing the last of my vodka redbull and glancing around the table. I haven't been paying much attention to the conversations around but the dynamic of the table shifted when they left.

Hayes, Everett, me, and four gorgeous women are left sitting at our table. *Oh, shit.* Everett is across from me with two girls on either side of him, laughing at whatever he says. The other two are sitting in middle booth, leaning as close to Hayes as they can. It's like watching group dates on 'The Bachelor' when the woman are fighting for just an ounce of attention.

The pit in my stomach only amplifies the longer I sit here. If Hayes didn't have his arm firmly around my shoulders, I'd already be on the dance floor with Dess. There's no way I can sit here and watch Hayes flirt with them. Yeah, he may have been a little more flirty toward me when I was his only option. Now? I don't stand a chance next to Double D Deb and Brazilian Butt Betty.

With every question they ask, they slowly inch closer to him and me by proxy. I feel like the opposite end of a magnet, trying to get away. He's not outright flirting with them, but he's not shutting them down either. Occasionally he tries to bring me into the conversation, but the more they talk, the more energy I lose to fight for his attention. No self-respecting woman should have to work this hard for a man's attention.

They all swap stories about living in Southern California, and the lifestyle they live. Brazilian Butt Betty is a fitness influencer like Heather is. She's practically started salivating when Hayes talked about his workout routine. Things I just don't care about anymore. Give me a mountain to hike or a trail to run on and I'm in. Kickboxing? Did it for years. But going to the gym daily to lift weights? Never been my thing.

The mortification I feel hits an all time high when Double D Deb reaches her hand out and runs her hot pink nail down his forearm. The music is loud, but not so loud that I can't hear her ask where he's staying and then invite herself to the suite. *Nope.*

I do what I do best. Bail.

Without a word, I get myself the hell out of that booth and down the stairs. No, goodbye; see ya later; I have to pee; nothing. One second I'm there and the next I'm jogging down the stairs in four inch wedges. Fuck Hayes. Fuck this night. Fuck social media influencers.

I weave my way through the dance floor, trying to get to the exit. It's dark, sweaty bodies are everywhere and I get shoved from side to side, but I'm not stopping. I'm mustering up whatever little confidence I have left and putting an end to my feelings toward Hayes. Even if that means cutting off conversation for a while. Cold turkey, or whatever.

I have a feeling everyone is going to give me shit for leaving without saying anything, but I don't give a damn. I'll text them when I get to the hotel and tell them I wasn't feeling well or some other believable excuse. All that I can think about is getting to the hotel first, locking myself in one of the rooms and sleeping with headphones on. Or. OR. I'll splurge and book my own suite at the hotel. The credit card bill is worth it to avoid the party that is being brought back to our room.

I slink past the bouncer at the front door, and start my fast-paced walk back to the hotel. It isn't far enough for a taxi, but walking alone in the middle of the night probably wasn't a good idea. Definitely will be getting a lecture in the morning. I'm not even twenty feet away from the club when I feel a large hand wrap around the inside of my arm and yank me back. Fight, flight, or freeze hits and my body always chooses fight.

I turn around, left arm poised to let my fist fly, only to pull it back at the last second. A very pissed off Hayes is shooting daggers at me through narrowed eyes.

"Where the fuck are you going, Charlotte?" Uh oh. Full name: he's pissed-pissed.

Feigning innocence seems like the most logical route right now. "Back to the hotel?"

"By yourself? What the fuck are you thinking?"

The huff that escapes me can only be described as guttural, mixed with annoyance. "I'm *leaving*. You're welcome to come or stay with your harlots, but I'm out."

I try to rip my arm out of his grip, but his grip only tightens. It's not enough to hurt, but enough that I'm not able to walk away as freely as I'd like without making a scene.

"Harlots?" His laugh shakes his entire chest. "Heather's friends? *Hell no.* I'd much rather go with you." He slides his hand down my arm and laces our fingers together.

We both start walking, letting the chill of the desert air fill our lungs and clear our heads. Despite the late hour, there's still people milling around, walking from hotel to hotel. The tension I felt earlier dissipates with each step we take away from the club, until I'm left feeling embarrassed for leaving how I did.

"Wanna tell me why you ran out of there like the place was on fire?"

I shake my head and grit my teeth. We both know that he knows exactly why. My pride can't handle any more dings with him, though, so I don't say anything at all.

"No? Anything to do with the 'harlots' trying to invite themselves to our suite?" I can tell he's trying to lighten the mood by teasing me but all it does is annoy me further. He's been hot and cold our entire adult lives, bringing me in and then pushing me away. It's my fault for holding onto a dream that someday we would be together. Him having his arm around me, while chatting up other girls was the push I needed.

"Nope. I know it's your birthday but if you could keep it down when they get there, I'd appreciate it."

I hear the undeniable sound of his teeth clenching together and then my arm is yanked backward. He spins me toward him so swiftly that I don't even stumble. The glow from the street lights behind him make him look both menacing and sexy.

"Sunshine. I'm going to say this once and only once. I don't give a damn about those women. Heather included for that matter. Every time they got closer to me, I leaned into you. I barely gave them half-ass answers to whatever bullshit question they asked me. If you weren't so busy ignoring me, you would've noticed."

My shoulders relax a touch with each word. "What do you want, Hayes? Because I've always only wanted *you*. If that's not what you want, let me *go*."

His head rears back like I slapped him. "Let *you* go? You've had me captivated for years. I can't remember the last time you weren't the first person on my mind in the morning, or the last when I went to bed. You're everything I've ever wanted and more. But, you're too damn good for me, Charlie. I'm terrified of fucking this up. Pushing you away somehow, losing you." He runs a hand through his hair and frowns. "You shouldn't be the wife sitting at home, waiting to see if her husband makes it back."

It feels like my eyebrows hit my hairline. I had no idea he had put half this much thought into us. But of course he had; Hayes has always been an over thinker.

"You mean like our moms? Who loved those husbands more than life itself? Loved the family they created together? You may have seen them as wives waiting at home, but I saw them as strong, resilient women who held everything together while their husbands were out there risking their lives."

The crease between his eyebrows grows as he looks down at me but he doesn't respond.

I reach out, cupping his face in my hand. "For you? I'd choose that worry, that dedication, and that love any day. I'd choose you above everything else."

His eyes soften as he finally meets mine, understanding the depth of my words. "I love you. I am *in* love with you."

Shock ripples through my body as I stare at him. "You are?"

"I am. Everett called me out before dinner in front of Drew. I thought he was going to be pissed, but instead he gave me his blessing. Felt like I won Gold at the Olympics. I was working up the nerve to kiss you all night."

"If I told you that I love you too, would that give you the final push?"

His eyes widen a fraction before he pulls me into him and kisses me. Searing his mouth to mine, my lips naturally part and I almost get dizzy. He tastes exactly as I thought he always would like peppermint and desire.

He pulls away too soon and leaves us both panting. "You love me, huh?" The wink he delivers at the end has me continually swooning. He's the definition of sexy and he doesn't even have to try.

Chuckling, I shove at his chest. "I do."

"Thank god." He grabs my hand again, pulling me the rest of the way to our hotel.

We both send out our quick, obligatory "we left" texts, as soon as we get into the suite. He lets go of my hand and jogs into the room that Odessa and I were staying in. I stand perfectly still where he left me, and within twenty seconds, he's marching out with my bag and taking it into his room.

I giggle and follow behind, standing in the doorframe. "How'd you know that was my bag?"

"Fifty/fifty shot. And my girl always travels light. Dess's bag looked like it could fit a small elephant," he says with a chuckle. *My girl? Swoon.*

He sets my bag down on the chaise and then turns so he's facing me. His dark eyebrow arches, clearly waiting for me to make the first move.

I step into the room, closing and locking the door behind me. It's been a while since the last time I hooked up with anyone. More than a while, actually. My love life has been drier than the Sahara. The way Hayes is looking at me, though, I have no doubt that's about to change. My only regret is not packing dirtier lingerie to tease him with.

When I turn back around, he's still standing where he was, but his entire demeanor has changed. Long gone is the playful Hayes. In his place is a predator who looks like he wants to devour me. Instead of making me nervous, though, it lights a fire of confidence inside of me. I slowly unzip the side of my dress and let it fall unceremoniously to the ground. His breath hitches while he stands there staring at me in only my pair of heels, a strapless bra, and a thong.

Those dark brown eyes slide down my body and then back up again. He runs his hand down his face while shaking his head and letting out a dry chuckle. "I'm so fucked. You're a goddamn vision, Sunshine."

In two large steps, he's standing in front of me, gripping my waist. He shakes his head, and a slow, devilish smirk spreads across his face. "We can go as fast or slow as you want tonight. Don't feel pressured—"

"Hayes, shut up and kiss me." And that's precisely what he does.

Chapter Five

Hayes

Light streams through the open curtains, casting a warm glow on the room. I guarantee it's closer to dinner than breakfast, but I'm not ready to get out of this bed yet. Not sure I'll ever be, to be honest.

Charlie and I didn't go to bed until well after the sun came up. Half of that time was spent all over each other, learning each other's bodies. The other half was spent laughing at ourselves for being too scared to tell each other how we felt. It felt like a hundred pound weight was lifted from my chest the second she said she loved me. The kiss that followed only sealed the deal. She's it for me. Always has been, always will be.

I've been awake for at least an hour, looking at Charlie with awe and disbelief. Not fully believing this beautiful, unattainable woman is mine and laying next to me. She's always been gorgeous but seeing her like this—freshly fucked with wild and untamed hair, smiling while she sleeps—gives an entirely new definition to the word perfect. There isn't much in life better than waking up to the girl of your dreams, naked, with one leg thrown over you. *The closest to Nirvana I'll ever get.*

Charlie groans as she stretches next to me but keeps her eyes closed. "Good morning, Carrington."

I tickle her sides while scoffing. "Carrington? I spent most of last night inside of you and now you're denouncing me to my last name?"

She giggles and nuzzles her face into my chest. "Sorry, handsome. How about, Good morning, 'man who rocked my world last night?'"

"Much better," I say, planting a kiss on the top of her head.

"So, you still love me? That wasn't all booze and hormones talking?" She asks with what sounds like a touch of nervousness.

The cutest gasp emits from her when I flip over her and settle myself on top of her. Holding myself up with my left arm, I gently cupped her face with my right hand. "Yes. You're beautiful, smart, funny, and have the biggest heart. I'd marry you right now if my mom wouldn't kill us both. Loving you was never my problem; being afraid that I wasn't good enough for you was."

"Says the guy who has threatened to burn the world down if someone hurt me." She gives me a pointed look and I grin.

"Not a threat, Sunshine. A promise. Together or not, I'd never let anyone hurt you."

Her eyes narrow a touch and she tilts her chin. "What do you mean together or not?"

With a sigh, I roll off of her and look at the ceiling. "We still have a lot to talk about. How we manage long-distance, what our plans are for the future, the impending deployment." *The lack of confidence I have in myself that I'm enough to keep you.*

"Okay. Let's start with the deployment. Drew mentioned it yesterday at the pool, so I already know a bit. Do you know when you're leaving?" She rolls over so that she has her leg thrown over me again. My body instantly relaxes when she starts tracing the lines of my abs.

"Not yet, could be a few months, could be a year. This is going to be..." I try to think of how to explain without worrying her or giving away anything classified. "It's not the standard; our team was selected to work on a discrete project. We'll be gone for at least a year. It could be more depending on the mission and how well we do."

"It's going to be dangerous. That's what you're not saying, right?" She squeezes her eyes shut and tries to turn away. I don't let her, though, keeping her pinned to me until she relaxes again.

"Drew and I are both ready for this. We've been trained, trained, and trained some more. You're more at risk living your normal life than we are."

She scoffs but at least she smiles. "Are you kidding? I'm kind of a badass myself. You just haven't been around enough to see me throw a punch."

I pull her chin back toward me and kiss her again. This time a little slower, a little more passion, like we have all the time in the world. At some point, we rolled back over so that I was on top of her again. This is how things went last night as well. We'd get into some deep conversations, only to get lost in each other's bodies before the conversation ended. She's the ultimate siren distraction.

When I break away again, I clarify what I meant. "I don't doubt you're a badass, but you shouldn't ever have to prove that. I'm only letting you know that you don't need to worry about me. I'll use the code dad and Uncle Jesse started with our moms to let you know where we are. Don't you dare stalk the news when you find out, but maybe it'll give you a little sense of peace." Our dads were gone so much that they came up with a system to tell our moms where they were. Different songs are for different regions of the world.

"Not sure about that, but I promise I won't do any deep-dives." Only the corner of her mouth tips up into a smile, but at least she isn't shying away anymore. "So, long-distance? Does that also tie into the 'our future' part?"

Nodding my head, I try once again to figure out how to delicately tell her my thoughts. "Long-distance is hard. Really fucking hard. I've seen more guys on deployment get broken up with, cheated on, and divorced than I can remember. They give us briefings on it at least once a month—how to handle a heartbreak without killing someone, basically. The culture that surrounds relationships in the military is scary. No one is loyal." With a deep breath, I continue. "All that being said, I don't want that to happen between us. I will do everything in my power to make sure you know how loved, appreciated, and dedicated I am to you, no matter the distance. I love you too much to lose you because you don't feel valued."

Tears well in her eyes as she nods. "I love you, too. I've waited ten years to be able to call you mine. Now that I have you, there's no way I'm going to let you go. You're it for me, Hayes. No one else could ever compare."

My heart swells with her words. I've wanted her for so long; hearing her say she feels the same is enough to get me through the next couple of years. I don't know if I'll renew my contract after this deployment, but I still have time to decide.

"Before I leave, though, I'm flying you out to me, or vice versa, at least twice a month. Phone calls, face times, sexting, the works. I want to talk to you all day, every day."

"Ooh, sexting? I'm intrigued. Tell me more about all the dirty things you're going to send to me."

"I'd rather show you so that when I text it to you later, you know *exactly* what I'm talking about."

I trace her bottom lip with my tongue and watch as her eyes darken with lust. She immediately grasped the back of my neck and drew me into a savage kiss. Kissing Charlie is like an electric shock running through my body; adrenaline spikes through me, chasing more ecstasy every time. It's easy to get lost in the moment, forgetting we are sharing a suite with our closest friends.

That is, until a loud knock, that sounds more like someone pounding sounds from the door. "Hey! Get out of bed, take a shower, and get dressed! You're not wasting the rest of our vacation locked in this hotel room." Odessa shouts while still banging.

"Dess, I love ya. But I really hate you right now!" I holler back. I was seconds away from being inside Charlie when Odessa's shitty timing had to ruin my moment again.

"Don't care! We've been waiting all day for you. We're hungry!"

Charlie chuckles underneath me and kisses my jaw before whispering, "We could finish this in the shower."

I've never moved as fast as I have at those words. Jumping out of bed, I lift her under her knees and carry her into the bathroom. She giggles the entire time and I want to bottle up the sound and keep it forever.

This trip, this moment, this connection—it's all I ever wanted in life but was too afraid to ask for. Charlie's it for me. She always has been, but now there's no denying it. This woman has wrecked me for all other women, there isn't any woman in the world that could come close to comparing to her.

Chapter Six

Hayes

Monday, March 6.

The team sits in the small conference room, twiddling our thumbs, waiting for the big news we are about to hear. It's almost a guarantee that our orders finally came in and they're sending us out. We've been working on specialized trainings the last few weeks, getting everything nailed down to perfection. My only hope is that our leave date isn't until June.

Charlie and I have been dating long-distance since my birthday. Every fiber of my being is madly in love with her. We visit each other as often as we can, call each other all the time, and text even more. I was worried about long-distance, but Charlie makes it easy. She's been staying busy with work and school still, but her graduation is at the end of May. The company she works for offered her a full-time position but she wasn't sure she would take it until she knew for sure when I was leaving. I have a feeling today is the day we've been dreading.

When the senior officers come in with grim expressions, everyone's shoulders sag at the same time. Some in relief, some in dread—all with the understanding we are deploying soon. The newer guys are eager to get out there and do what we've been training to do. Those of us who have done it a few times know exactly what to expect. A shitstorm of fighting a battle that never seems to end and the realization that not everyone in this room may come back.

"Eight weeks. Mosul, Iraq. There will be three other teams working in the area, but our objectives are not the same. You aren't to be seen or heard." I'm not surprised to hear that. Our team is designed to be different. To be the best.

I can feel Drew staring at me but I simply shake my head once. Neither of us are the most terrific at math, but we both know that 'eight weeks' means we won't be making it to South Carolina for Charlies graduation or birthday. They fall close to the same weekend and we already had our flights booked.

The hardest part is that I know she's going to be devastated but won't show her emotions to me. She'll throw on a brave face for me, and then cry when we get off the phone so that it doesn't add to my mental load.

The phone rings and rings and rings, each ring grating on my nerves. I've been trying to call Charlie all day, but she's been in and out of classes. We've missed each other every time and the nerves of telling her have only grown to a suffocating level.

Finally, her sweet voice answers. "Hayes! Babe, I miss you! Sorry we've been playing phone tag all day. It's been so chaotic here between classes and work."

"It's okay," I say as I crunch through a mint. I wish I could muster up some more enthusiasm, but I hate disappointing Charlie and I know it's coming.

"What's wrong?" This woman knows me better than anyone else. The first sentence I've spoken and she's already onto me.

I took a deep breath and then puffed out my cheeks when I let it out. "We received our orders this morning."

The line goes deadly silent as she starts to absorb what that means. "Shit."

I nod, despite that she can't see it. "Eight weeks."

Her sharp inhale is the only thing that gives her true feelings away. "Okay, well, okay. One year is a drop in the bucket. Right?" *Problem-solving mode, like she needs to convince me it's okay.*

My shoulders sag slightly. "It is. But I'm going to miss your birthday and graduation." I wish I could be there to pull her into my arms. I should be the one reassuring her. Not the other way around.

"Oh." The mask has already started slipping, disappointment weaving its way into her voice.

"I'm so sorry, Sunshine."

"It's not your fault. Your mom will be there, as will Odessa. One of them can send you a video."

My throat feels clogged with emotion as she keeps assuring me that everything will be okay. "Thanks; I'd love to see it."

Add this to the list of milestones I have to miss out on. The sacrifices never felt as daunting when I wasn't disappointing Charlie. I know it's a struggle that everyone in the military has to deal with, but that doesn't make it any easier. Even our dad's couldn't handle the time away. Once they missed a few birthdays, family vacations, and holidays, they decided it wasn't worth it. I get it now. How hard it must have been for them to finish their contracts, because all I want to do is break mine.

Charlie

Tears stream down my face as I sit in my car outside of my apartment. Hayes just called to let me know he can't make it to my college graduation and he'll be off to whatever war-torn country they send him to. I want to be mad and sad and throw a giant fit but it won't change anything. This is the life I'll have to get used to if I want to be with Hayes. The life I told him that I could handle. Just like our mom's did.

Finally, I get out of my car and start walking toward my apartment. This complex is huge, with each floor having four apartments. I've lived here for about a year and I'm the newest one on the second floor. The neighbor across from me must be a nurse, because I rarely see her and when I do, she's always in scrubs. The neighbor next to me, Carter, is a single guy who is pretty quiet but always smiles and says hi when he sees me. In the apartment across from him lives a single mom with two teenage kids. The kids can be a little rowdy but the mom is always very polite and apologetic. I don't mind them, though; they remind me of Drew and me. Always bickering, but the love is there.

Carter happens to be walking toward our building at the same time as I am. He's carrying a massive bouquet of flowers that he can barely see over. When he notices that it's me next to him, he smiles and stops walking. "Hey, Charlotte!"

"Hey. Some bouquet you have there. They're beautiful!"

His entire face light's up at my compliment. "They are, aren't they? My grandmother has quite the garden." A wistful expression takes over his face as he looks at them. Then he plucks out a white rose and hands it to me. "These are my favorite though. They've always reminded me of my favorite person."

I try to control my eyebrows from hitting my hairline, but everything about that sentence gives me the heebie-jeebies and

I don't know why. "Yeah... Well, they are lovely," I say with a polite smile.

He takes a second to adjust the flowers and then his eyes widen when he takes a better look at me. "Woah, Charlotte. Are you okay? You look like you've been crying."

He reaches his free hand to touch my arm as he takes a step closer to me. My instincts naturally put the distance back between us as I step away, nodding my head. The optics of how this would look to Hayes aren't beyond me. A seemingly random guy giving me flowers? Not a good look. Especially to a man who already has a lot of stress on his mind.

"I'm okay. I just got some bad news." I say as I start to walk up the stairs, hoping to avoid talking anymore about this. It doesn't feel right for me to cry on another man's shoulder. Especially considering I just told Hayes how I was fine with the demands of his job.

"Do you want to talk about it?" His shaggy hair covers his light blue eyes and he keeps trying to push it back with his free hand. He gives off frat boy mixed with surfer vibes, wearing his dark jeans and a polo.

I shake my head and take another step. "No, thanks, though. I just need a shower and some sleep. See ya around."

He smiles back but something seems off about it, like he's disappointed. I've never gotten a bad feeling from him, but he always has an intense energy surrounding him. As if he's reading into everything I say, looking for a deeper meaning.

I make my way into my apartment, locking the door behind me.

I half-drop and half-set my purse on the table by the door. It lands with a thud, sounding louder than normal in my quiet little apartment. Taking a look around, the realization hits me that I'll have to renew my lease for another year. I always liked this apartment but I was really hoping I would get to spend some time in San Diego with Hayes before he left. Even if it had only been a few weeks, I wanted that time with him to just be and live. Spending long weekends together has been amazing, but it's only made me want more. More time. More love. More Hayes.

Chapter Seven

Charlie

"Charlie, listen to me. Hayes loves you. Everyone knows Hayes loves you. He's borderline obsessed with you. I swear to you that you are overthinking this entire thing." Odessa has been listening to me fret over Hayes being distant for a few weeks now. She's answered every call, talked me off the ledge, and given me the pep talk of all pep talks. Still, my gut is telling me something is off. Every time we talk, which isn't as often as it once was, he's distant and distracted. It feels like the Hayes from eight months ago, before we were dating.

"Even though I told him I would fly out and he made up some excuse why he couldn't see me? I know he's lying, Dess." Hayes leaves in a handful of days and I offered to fly out to spend a week there before he left. I assumed that he would be busy, but only twenty minutes of face-to-face would have been worth it to me. He said he wouldn't even have that much time, though. A big fat lie considering Heather let it slip that she and Drew have plans because the guys have a four day weekend.

"I know. I'm not saying that his lying to you is okay. But I don't think it's as sinister as you think it is. He's been telling you how concerned he is about this deployment and what it will do to your relationship. I think you might have to be the strong one right now. Show him you're with him throughout it all. Allow him to be the one to spiral for a change, and trust him when he says that he loves you. Ya know?" *Dammit.* She makes a point. I can't begin to imagine the stress he is under and I don't want to add to it by constantly doubting him.

"You're right." I say with a grumble. "Wait! Since when are you the voice of reason? Shouldn't you be booking us plane tickets to slash his tires?"

She chuckles in the background. "If it were any man other than Hayes, yes. However, he has the best heart of all of us. He'd never intentionally do anything to hurt you."

"Yeah, yeah." I sigh into the phone. It's loud on her end of the phone; people are chattering in the background but she doesn't seem to be in a hurry to get off the phone. "How's life on the road? Where even are you?"

"Exhausting. I have a couple more days in NYC and then I'll be home for a week in between gigs. I need the reprieve that only mom can offer." Odessa has been calling Connie "mom" since she moved in with us at fifteen. Despite the reputation their last name holds, the Astors have never been stellar parents. If anything, the money only made them more neglectful and abusive. Connie's house became all of our safe house and thankfully she had enough love to go around for all of us.

"That'll be good. Mind if I come home too? I promise to not complain about Hayes the whole time."

"You better be there. I'll bring the wine; you bring the snacks." Red flags go off in my mind when I realize her voice lacks the lightness it normally carries.

"Everything okay? You sound off."

"Yeah, just tired. I gotta get on set. See ya this weekend!"

She hangs up the phone before I can say anything else. Her telltale sign something is wrong and she's not ready to talk about it. Odessa has always been an outstanding advice-giver but she hates to be vulnerable herself. She has that in common with Hayes. The two of them shut down when they need to process their emotions and I know that I need to give them the space to do so, but I can't help but feel a bit helpless in the meantime.

I stared at the dark screen of my phone for a little while after we ended the call. Replaying what Odessa said about Hayes, wondering what she has going on that has her sounding so down, and trying to decide what to do with the rest of my evening. I've been living alone for a few years now but never have I felt this lonely.

Instead of calling Hayes out on his lack of communication, I take Odessa's advice—choosing faith in our relationship over doubt. I send him a quick "I miss you" text and add a picture of us from Vegas that I haven't ever shown anyone. Our first picture as a couple—a selfie of us in bed. Everything is covered but you can clearly tell what we have been up to. It's the happiest I've ever seen Hayes look and I'm hoping it'll remind him of that as well. The pep talk that Odessa just gave me was enough to keep me from spiraling into a mess of self-doubt, but I still feel the pang of sadness in my chest when he doesn't respond right away. Leaving things unsaid and unsettled is not my style, but I trust that Hayes will come around in his own time. I'll give him the space he needs, knowing that our connection is strong enough to withstand a little distance.

Sighing, I leave my phone on the table and start cleaning my apartment. It's minimalist, with barely any furniture, but I never minded before. I've been focused on finishing school early, working, and, Hayes, not decorating an apartment I hadn't planned on living in for very long. Now that my plans have changed, I make a mental note of all the things I should buy to add a little more personality to the space. Maybe a colorful rug, some throw pillows, and a couple plants could liven up the place. As I scrub the floors and dust the empty shelves, I can't help but feel a sense of determination to make this apartment feel like home.

First things first, I need to go through my bedroom at Connie's this weekend and find some things to bring here. I swear every square inch of that room has memories in it—from family photos from before my parents died to new ones of Hayes and me, it's like a walk down memory lane every time I step foot in there. It shouldn't be surprising that I've felt so unsettled in this apartment; I don't have anything personal here. Connie's house is still "home" to me, despite that I haven't lived there in a few years. It's where I go on the weekends when I'm feeling alone or down. Connie and I always had a strong relationship, but living with her alone for so many years really solidified it. She became my best friend and if I'm being honest with myself, a crutch to deal with the loneliness. That's some-thing I need to work on while Hayes is gone—being okay with feeling lonely and finding ways to fulfill that void on my own.

Chapter Eight

Hayes

Friday, April 28.

Weeks and weeks of emails, texts, and long phone calls had led up to this moment. I had Charlie convinced I wouldn't be able to make it to see her before I deployed next week. Somehow, by the mercy of God and the US Navy, I was approved for a four-day weekend to see my girl.

The second I was off work on Thursday, I was heading to the San Diego airport to catch my overnight flight to Atlanta. One more flight will have me in Columbia, where my mom and Odessa will pick me up. She happened to be in town, which is perfect for the second big surprise I have planned.

Everything so far has gone exactly as planned, and I'm in my old truck heading to Charlie's work to surprise her. She was able to visit for spring break, but that already feels like a lifetime ago. Leaving for a year is going to be harder than we both anticipated.

I stand outside her swanky office building and lean against her front bumper on the Ford Explorer we picked out together.

We spent hours searching online for the right fit, and I flew out here to help her test drive cars last year. As I wait for her to finish work, memories flood through my mind. Her trips to see me, my visits home, and the weekend in Vegas that changed everything. Any free moment I've had, which aren't many, I've spent with her. Every good moment I've had somehow involves her. She's become my everything. My soulmate. The one my heart beats for.

I run my finger over the smooth tin in my pocket. The box normally only has mints in it, but right now it's holding something considerably more cherished. We've only been officially dating for a little over eight months, but I've never been as sure of anything as I am of Charlie. I don't want to leave without promising a future to her. She deserves it all, the ring, a house, kids. I want to be the one to make all of her dreams come true.

She walks out and waves goodbye to a shorter, blonde woman. The woman smiles back and turns to go in the opposite direction. Assumedly, her coworker Ava.

I bide my time, waiting for her to see me. The smirk on my face only grows wider as I watch her dig in her purse, completely oblivious to me waiting for her.

"Hey, Sunshine!" I hollered, getting her attention, when I finally couldn't handle it anymore.

Her gaze snaps up, and she drops her purse at the sight of me.

Sprinting across the parking lot, she leaps into my open arms and encircles her legs around my waist.

No words. She only seals those perfect lips to my mouth while I hold her to me.

"What are you doing here?" She mumbles along my lips.

"Had to see you before I left. I'm sorry I've been so distracted the last few weeks, I wanted to get everything done and I was afraid I'd ruin the surprise if I said too much."

She nods, kissing me again before I set her down and jogged over to pick up her forgotten purse.

Bringing it back, I hand it to her. "Should we drop your car off at home and grab some dinner?"

She kisses me once more and nods. "Let's go."

We head to our usual Thai place, just down the road. Not only is it our favorite, but it's also quick and still close to her apartment. We sit next to each other in a booth by the window, and I pull her close to me. There aren't enough hours left in the weekend for her to be anywhere but right next to me.

"Is it okay that I surprised you? I'm not interrupting anything, am I?" I ask, trying to gauge her reaction to me ruining whatever weekend plans she may have had. Normally, she isn't a big fan of surprises, either. She's all about the buildup of anticipation and the excitement that comes with it.

She grabs my thigh and flashes her pearly whites at me. "You're the best surprise. If all my surprises were you, I'd never want to know what's coming again."

Smiling back, I say, "Good. I'm glad."

"And to answer your other question, you're not interrupting anything. Finals are coming up, so I planned on shutting myself in and studying. However, spending the weekend in bed with you will be much more fun." She raises her eyebrows suggestively, but I'm still hung up on finals. In all the excitement, I'd forgotten she should be studying for her classes. She's been working so hard to get over a 4.0; I don't want to be the reason she doesn't get it.

I open my mouth to say something, but she cuts me off. "Don't you give me that worried look, Hayes. I've been studying for months. Anything now is just reaffirming what I already know. I have every day *after* you leave to look through my notes."

I nodded and swallowed the guilt I was feeling. Charlie has

always been a no-bullshitter, even when it comes to me. If she needed to study, she would tell me.

"Good, because I plan on occupying your entire weekend. You have UberEats or Doordash? Because I'm hoping this is the last time we leave the apartment until Sunday evening."

Her chin tips slightly to the left. "Sunday evening?"

"I told mom that we'd come to dinner."

She swats my chest. "Hayes! You have to see her more than just that! I can't hog you the whole time."

"Nope, I saw her this morning and we had breakfast. Odessa is in town for a little while too, so they already had plans." My mom, of all people, knows how important it is for us to have our own time. She was on the other side of my dad's deployments and Navy career for years.

We ate our food in record time, both feeling the need to get out of here without saying it. I paid and hustled her back out to my old truck.

It's still light out when we get back to her apartment, giving us an ample amount of time left in our evening. I haven't decided when to propose yet, but it'll be soon. She insisted that she doesn't want a big, flashy proposal, but I want it to at least be romantic.

I rush around the truck to open her door and hold her hand as we walk up the steps to her apartment. It's a decent place, a safe neighborhood, and it has a gate in the front that only residents have a code for. It's one less thing for me to worry about while gone. I'd lose my damn mind if she was living anywhere unsafe. Columbia doesn't have a lot of crime, but that doesn't mean it's without risk.

She puts the key in the lock and then pauses to look at me. "I'm so happy you're here."

I give her a quick kiss and smack her on the ass. "Let's go, Sunshine. I need you naked in the next five seconds."

She giggles and opens the door, and as it swings open, the scent of roses drift out into the hall.

She looks at me with wide eyes and a small smile. "Hayes, what is all this?!"

Shrugging my shoulders, I say, "It wasn't me."

Her mouth drops, and as she steps inside, white roses cover the entire apartment. Every inch is completely covered in roses—petals, buds, and full-bloom bouquets.

I step in front of her and walk into the apartment, trying to figure out who did this. Odessa knew I was in town, but she didn't mention anything about it. Neither did my mom.

The rustling noise of a bed frame moving sounds from the bedroom and then I hear it. A male voice shouts her name, beckoning to her. *What the fuck?*

My heart stops as my head slowly turns to her. Her face is drained of all of its color; long gone is the carefree smile from earlier.

Two large steps into her room have me face-to-face with a man that I've never seen before. He's wearing a cheap suit and holding a rose in his hand. His back leans against her headboard like he's been in here a million times.

His head jerks back, and his forehead creases when he sees me. He sits up and moves to the edge of the bed. Throwing his hand out at me like I'm the intruder. "Who the fuck are you?"

"Me? Who the fuck are *you*?" I don't give him a second to respond. I know who he is—the man fucking my girl.

I slam my fist into his nose and hear the deafening crunch of bone. It does nothing to relieve my temper, so I yank him up by the lapels of his jacket and throw him into the wall parallel to her bed. His head bobbles slightly as he slinks down it.

Blood gushes out of his nose, already landing on the stark white petals covering the floor.

Rage pulses through my veins as I stare at him slumped on

the floor. I know that if I don't leave this room, I'll kill him. As much as I want nothing more than to let my wrath take over, I've been trained to know when to stop.

Turning on my heels to leave, I storm past Charlie.

She looks terrified of me, but I don't spare her more than a glance. She's the cause of all this. It's nothing new for military personnel to get cheated on—it happens all the time. They give us fucking briefings on how to handle it. I never expected Charlie to do that to me, though.

I take the stairs two at a time as I rush out of the building.

The adrenaline carrying me to my truck—I've been conditioned to thrive on this feeling. Working on instinct rather than emotion. I need to get as far away from the situation as possible.

Chapter Nine

Charlie

I ran after him down the steps of my apartment building, grabbing his arm to get him to stop walking.

"Hayes! Are you kidding me? You honestly think I would cheat on you?"

He looks at me with such vitriol and disgust that you'd think he just walked in and saw me having sex with Carter.

My heart is beating so hard that it feels like an out-of-body experience. He can't see past his arrogance to realize that maybe he's wrong and that I didn't have anything to do with Carter being in my apartment. For fuck's sake, I've barely said more than a dozen sentences to this creep but Hayes won't let me explain that.

The realization that he doesn't trust me hits me like a freight train. I knew that he struggled with anxiety from his previous deployments and seeing his teammates be cheated on left and right. Even still, he jokes with me about all the briefings on how to handle separations while deployed. He always made it sound like he trusted me though, trusted us. The way he's looking at me makes it feel like that was all one carefully constructed lie to hide his true thoughts.

"I'm not cheating on you! I swear to you that I had no idea he was up there." Anger mixes with hurt until I'm yelling at him. I haven't done anything for months but focus on Hayes, on us, and on our future. I go to school, go to work, and talk to him. *Yet, I'm the bad guy?!*

"So what, Charlie? He just broke into your apartment?! Covered it in flowers as some grand gesture for no reason? Men don't do that shit for nothing!"

Gasping for air, it feels like he just knocked the wind out of me. *Is he seriously gaslighting me right now?* Being friendly toward a man is reason enough for him to break into my apartment? He's doubting me because of his insecurities, and I haven't done anything to deserve that.

"Fuck *you*, Hayes! Don't you dare blame me for this!"

He threw his arms out to the side, his face twisting with anger. He honestly thinks I invited Carter into my house and I've been having an affair with my neighbor.

"You wouldn't be the first chick to cheat on her deployed boyfriend. You probably won't be the last."

My heart sinks at his words, denouncing me as just another "chick."

He's never once made me feel anything but extraordinary. Today, though, he's making me feel like I'm nothing, like we haven't shared years of friendship that turned into love.

"You know," he laughs harshly. "Usually the women wait until we're at least out of the country! You've always been an overachiever, though, huh?"

"Hayes! I would *never!*" Somewhere between the shock and anger I'm feeling toward him not believing me, there's a scared girl trying to make him believe her.

He doesn't care anymore, though. It's written all over his face before he turns and walks away.

He throws open his driver door, and the metal groans in protest as he gets into his truck. Without a second glance, he's speeding away. I stare at the back of the truck with blurry vision as sobs rake through my body. The truck we've spent countless hours making memories in. The truck that I would sit in when he left for boot camp just to feel close to him.

As I watch him drive off, a sense of emptiness fills me. The foundation of our relationship shattered in an instant and I'm left questioning everything we've ever had together.

I'll never understand how he could just leave me here like this. Completely and utterly broken. I thought he was my everything, my best friend, and my future. But how can he be all of those things when he wouldn't listen to my side of things before jumping to conclusions.

I walk back up the steps, remembering there's one more problem to deal with.

Carter.

I've never been anything more than polite to him. Not once have I led him on or even invited him into my apartment. I don't even know how he got in. I would have sworn the door was locked, but now I can't remember if I heard the lock click when I unlocked the door tonight.

My apartment doesn't look like mine anymore. The white roses are everywhere. It looks like my living room is covered in snow. Snow and a trail of blood from where Carter must have run out of here. I should have known the second I saw those roses that it was him. My gut was telling me that him giving me that rose the other day was creepy, but I ignored it. *A mistake I won't be making again.*

I don't have any sympathy for him, or his blood loss; he crossed a major line.

Grabbing my phone, I call the only person I can trust.

"Dess. I need you."

It only took Odessa thirty minutes to get here from Heartsville. So it's safe to assume she broke every speeding law there was. One more reason to be thankful for my "don't give a fuck attitude" best friend.

"Holy shit." She looks around the room, staring at the glaring whiteness of it all. "I take it this wasn't Hayes?"

A sob that sounds like a laugh comes out of my chest as I shake my head. "My neighbor, Carter. I've barely talked to him, Dess! He was in my *bed*. Why would he do this?"

She whips out her phone and immediately calls 911. She doesn't ask any more questions, taking charge of the situation like an older sister would.

"Hello. I need an officer for Palmetto Apartment #138. There's been a break-in."

She nods and answers more questions, but I can't stand to be in here anymore. I half-walk and half-run back outside to sit in my car.

Within a few minutes, an officer arrives and starts asking questions. So, so many questions. Questions that I don't have the answer to.

"What's his last name?" Don't know.

"How'd he get in?" Don't know.

"Why did he do this?" Don't know.

"How long have you been friends with him?" Friends with him? I've talked to him in passing a handful of times.

"Have you led him on in any way?" I want to say, "Hell fucking no!" But, at this point, I'm exhausted and confused. I don't know if my being polite fed into whatever delusion he had or if he's just insane. All that I know is that I never want to see him again. Or white fucking roses.

After an hour of questions by three different officers, they basically tell me they can't do anything but file a report. One of them even goes so far as to say to me, "Don't worry, your apartment is safe to go back into now." *Is it? Is it really Officer Goodwin? Because, I thought it was safe a few hours ago, and then I found a delusional person in my bed!*

I lost my boyfriend, best friend, and future in a matter of minutes because I was friendly to the wrong person, and there's nothing anyone can do about it, not even the police.

Chapter Ten

Charlie

Friday, May 12.

"**R**eally, Char—I don't have to go. I can stay as long as you need me." Odessa hasn't left my side for the last two weeks. She was there for every tear, every breakdown, and every moment of anxiety I'd had. Not only was my safe place taken advantage of, but the man I love walked out of my life. Slamming the door behind him and locking it as he left.

"You do. I have finals to take, and you need to get back to New York. I'll be okay." I say, trying to convince Odessa as well as myself. She has a huge campaign coming up, which could be career-changing. I can't be the one to hold her back from this dream.

She nods and places her arms around my shoulders. She's always towered over me, my 6-foot-tall best friend, and she's been the pillar of strength for me more times than I can count. If it wasn't Hayes, it was Dess. *Now apparently, it's only Dess.*

"Call me. Anytime. Please."

Nodding, I let her go.

I need to stand strong, on my own.

Carter told the police that he thought I was interested in him, and in some grand gesture, he was trying to win me over. It's like he stole the words from Hayes' mouth. They seemed skeptical but told me their hands were tied. It's infuriating that on all fronts I'm the one getting blamed for someone breaking into my apartment.

Hayes won't answer my calls, emails, or texts. He's successfully blocked me from everything and completely shut me out of his life. I've even tried to call Drew, but he's pretty much taken Hayes' side and won't let me explain. He's short and distant with each phone call, and all it does is enrage me. I want to slam my fist into both of their noses. The abandonment and betrayal hit me hard, and I let it. I need something to fuel the anger that I want to feel. I don't want to be scared anymore, I want to be ruthless.

D**evoting** every spare minute to studying, making sure I'm eating enough food, and not thinking about Hayes has been exhausting. I've avoided Carter like the plague, and luckily he's been doing the same. My apartment door stays locked at all times, and I do a small perimeter check the second I walk through the door. *No psychos in my bed or hiding in closets here.*

With every passing day, I start to feel safe again, and begin to think that maybe Carter isn't actually psychotic. I haven't seen him since the incident, and my apartment is starting to feel normal again. I'm trying to convince myself that it really may have just been some weird grand gesture. A very creepy, over-the-line gesture, but still, maybe not as dangerous as I initially thought.

My phone rings, and I see it's Ava. She was one of Hayes and mines biggest supporters, giving me as much time off as I wanted to visit him. When I told her what happened with Carter she was both equally pissed off at Hayes and Carter.

"Hey, Av's. What's up?" I ask as I answer her call.

"Oh my gosh! I'm so glad you answered. I know you are swamped with finals and it's a Saturday, but is there any way I can get you to the office? The Barnaby's just moved the deadline to Monday morning, and Noah needs to review everything before he submits it. He's losing his mind right now because he has to be on a flight by 3:30. I need these docs proofed, scanned, and sent to him in the next two hours, and I'm only a third of the way done."

"I'll be right there." I say, grabbing my keys and sliding my feet into my vans. I usually go for a more professional appearance in the office, but it sounds like Ava's drowning in paperwork and needs me now.

I make it to the office in under ten minutes and get right to work helping proof a stack of documents.

"Thank you so much. You have no idea how stressed I was."

I grin back. "All good. I was just sitting on my couch anyway. I needed a break from reading over the same notecards a million times."

She laughs, "That feels like a lifetime ago for me. I don't miss the stress one bit."

One eyebrow raises on its own toward her. "This job is a thousand times more stressful than any class I've ever taken."

"True, but at least the money makes it all worth it."

She's got a good point there; Noah pays well above what anyone else in the industry would. I'm lucky that I even got the job, considering my lack of experience. I'm pretty sure it was only because my brother and Hayes played football with his younger brother when they were in high school. Being from the same small town gave me a very small connection with Noah, and I made sure to leverage that link during the interview process. Maybe more than leverage. I exploited the heck out of it.

"Think Noah's still reeling that the deadline got pushed up?" I ask as she finishes scanning the last document.

"You have no idea. He was using his growly voice at me as if I were the one who changed it."

"He only uses that tone with you. Everyone else uses his business-professional tone or his angry, 'you're fired' tone."

She rolls her eyes, but I see a small smile. "I've been here for so long that I think he knows I won't take it personally."

"Mhm, sure. You're also the only one I've ever seen him smile at."

She pauses mid-typing, her eyes flicking to mine. "It's not like that. I'm just his assistant."

I nod and try to give her a reassuring smile. "Okay, well, if that ever changed, you've got my vote. He is H. O. T., hot."

Her eyes widen just a fraction, and then she's laughing. "You're not wrong. I love my job, though. I wouldn't want to jeopardize that, even if there *was* something."

"I get that. It's hard to jump headfirst into something that will change the dynamic you're already used to."

Her shoulders sag just a fraction and she nods once. "How are you holding up? Everything still quiet around the apartment?"

Ava was one the first people I called after the incident. She showed up to my apartment, helped calm me down, and then gave me a few days off of work so that I could go stay at Connies. She must have filled Noah in as well, because my first day back, he called me into his office. I thought for sure he was firing me, but instead he gave me his personal cell phone number to call if I needed anything. It was the first time he'd acknowledged me in a personal way, and I almost cried right there. The whole situation felt a lot more real now that the always-stoic Noah was offering his help.

"It's been quiet. I haven't seen or heard from Carter since that night. If it weren't for the fact that Hayes isn't talking to me, I would've thought the whole thing was a dream."

Her eyes fill with sympathy as she looks at me. "I'm sorry. Men can be such morons sometimes. Can't see what's right there in front of them."

"Yeah, they've already left too. Drew, at least, sent me an email to let me know. He's giving me a pretty good cold shoulder right now." It's always been his go-to when things get complicated. He gives me enough conversation to let me know he's still alive, but not so much that he has to actually engage with me.

Ava lets me continue to rant, knowing I need to get it all out. "He's such an asshole. I'm the only family he has left and he won't even hear my side. And Hayes? He blocked me! Everything I send bounces back. I'm so pissed off but at the same time, it's killing me that he left thinking I would cheat on him."

"You can't control what other people choose to believe. Do you think there's more going on with him? A reason that he would jump to that conclusion so quickly?"

"Yeah, I know there is. The guys on his team get cheated on all the time." It's the culture that surrounds them. They spend so much time together, in high-risk situations, under constant pressure. He's told me how hard it is to rely on people outside of his team. When he's deployed, those are pretty much the only people he can trust. When they're home, the circum-stances change but the wariness doesn't. Apparently I fall under the "can't be trusted" category. The shittiest part is that I haven't done anything for him to have trust issues. That's all the U.S. Navy and whatever cheating hoes his teammates are with.

Ava reaches out and touches my arm, bringing me out of my thoughts. "I'm so sorry, Charlie. Idiots, all of them."

A small laugh escapes; she's spot on. Hayes, my brother, Carter. Even Noah for not going after Ava. All a bunch of idiots.

Chapter Eleven

Hayes

Friday, May 26.

Up, down, up, down.

My biceps and lats have been burning for the last forty-five chin-ups, but I've been pushing through. I need the physical pain to take away the emotional pain. I've done a good job shutting out the world back home, but today is different. Today is Charlie's birthday. I haven't spoken to her in over a month—not since I surprised her and we walked into her apartment only to find it covered in flowers.

I don't think I'll ever get over the betrayal I felt seeing some guy in her bed, waiting for her. His stunned face still haunts me. She must not have mentioned that she had a boyfriend to him. Just like she didn't mention that she had a side piece to me. Hell, maybe I was the side piece.

The crunching sound of his nose giving out didn't give me as much gratification as I was hoping it would. Looking back, I should've gone for more. Especially considering somehow in the scuffle my dad's tin box fell out of my pocket. My past and future vanished in the span of forty-five seconds. Right now, I'm not sure which one I'm more pissed off about losing.

Up, down, up, down. My movements are getting slower but I haven't stopped yet.

All that I can think about is that Charlie fucking broke me. Me. The guy who should be invincible. Broken by a woman who I trusted more than anyone in the world.

I don't know how she could lie behind my back and then directly to my face, but the proof was right there. In her bed.

I left for my third deployment only a handful of days later, and I've done everything I can to push her to the back of my mind. I eat, work, workout, and sleep. I blocked her on everything when I got to the airport that evening. I didn't even go to see my mom; I knew she would only make excuses, and I couldn't listen. If Drew hadn't been in our condo when I got back, I probably wouldn't have told him. He dragged it out of me, though, so I told him the basics. She was cheating on me, and I flew home. After that, I shut down completely. I don't want to see, hear, or talk about Charlie.

But that doesn't stop me from missing her. I miss her more than I thought possible. Her laugh and phone calls, her uncanny ability to turn my shitty mood into a good one. All that sunshine she brought to my dark days.

"Carrington!" Lincoln, a guy on my team, walks out to the makeshift gym. He's on the smaller side, a little nerdy, and smart as hell. "The fuck are you still doing? You want to be able to lift your arms tomorrow? You need to quit."

I grunt, but keep lifting myself up. I can handle a lot more than this.

Drew walks out behind him and when he sees me, he sighs. "It's my sister's birthday."

Lincoln nods. "Ahhh, letting the cheating ex get into your head."

I drop down from the bar, rage filling my body. "Don't fucking talk about her."

His grin back tells me he accomplished just what he wanted—me off the pull-up bar.

"Easy, Tiger. I'll drop it. Time to get your shit together. You can't be thinking about home here. It's a big one. A lot of moving parts. If your head is back there, you might as well be back there too."

"Is that a threat?" He isn't our team leader, but he has enough rank that he could easily get me pulled from here.

"For fuck's sake." He throws his hands in the air and sits on the bench. "This isn't about you. I can't, in good conscience, allow you or anyone to jeopardize what we have going on. I'm not trying to threaten you, but I need you to understand the gravity of this shit. The only way we all get through this tour unscathed is if everyone is fully committed."

"I'm working out. Not crying in my fucking bunk. Mind your business." I walk out of the makeshift gym and toward the shower. A hazy rage lingers over me as I stew over the bullshit he was spewing.

For the first time since I've been here, I let myself think about Charlie and now everyone is on my case, like they have nothing better to do. Which I guess, they don't. Today, every-thing is quiet. Too fucking quiet. Everyone is getting antsy to do something—to do whatever the hell we came here to do. Sitting on our asses all day and twiddling our thumbs ain't it.

After I've cooled down a bit, I realize he's not wrong. I let myself dive back into my feelings and lost my focus, even for the brief amount of time it was. Things go from calm sea to shitstorm in a matter of minutes here; I can't lose sight of that. I thought our last deployment felt dangerous; this one has ten times the pressure. One slip-up, and the entire world is on our ass or we are dead. Possibly both.

I can think about Charlie when I'm stateside.

Figure out where we went wrong.

Why I wasn't enough.

How I go about life without her.

Chapter Twelve

Charlie

Monday, May 29.

"Bye, Ava!" I called out as I waved goodbye. We worked our butts off today, but it felt good.

Today was the best day I've had in weeks, and I don't have an exact reason. Maybe it's that I'm finally a college graduate or that I'm starting to feel like I have a purpose. Maybe it's that my 21st birthday was a few days ago and I'm still excited for the milestone and the bottle of wine I just picked up. Either way, I'm grateful for the positive uptick in emotions.

I turn the volume up on my drive home, blaring 'I'm an Albatroz' by AronChupa and Little Sis Nora. It's silly. It's fun. It's got a good enough beat that I won't cry into my Ben and Jerry's when I get home. Most importantly, though, it doesn't remind me of Hayes.

Before I get out of the car, I search the stairs and parking lot, looking for any signs of Carter. I haven't seen him in weeks, but I still try to avoid any awkward run-ins. I'm just praying that I get that raise and can move out of here soon. I'm not as scared or angry anymore, but I still don't want anything to do with him. He's the reason Hayes and I aren't together anymore, and for that, he's as good as dead to me.

Getting out of my car, I make it up the flight of stairs and unlock the door. Now, I always listen for the deadbolt to click before I touch the handle. I slam the door behind me and deadbolt it again as soon as I'm inside.

I take a deep breath as I lean on the door and scan over every inch of the living room and kitchen. *Not as scared, my ass.*

Nothing is out of place, as it hasn't been since that one incident.

With a sigh, I throw my purse on the little table by the door and then make my way into the living room. Flipping on the TV as I go, torturing myself with the news. I leave the noise on in the background, praying I never hear any mention of Navy SEALs. I don't even know where Hayes and Drew are, but that doesn't stop me from stressing over every war-torn country.

My fridge is nearly empty, but for once, I'm actually hungry. I grab an uncrustable out of the freezer to thaw. At this point, I don't care what I'm eating. Any calorie to keep myself from getting low blood sugar and passing out is fine with me.

"BREAKING NEWS: USS Fitzbarell Naval Ship," a newscaster announces from the living room. My stomach sinks as I race around the counter to see what's going on.

"Collided with a container ship early this morning. Five sailors appear to be missing, and multiple injuries have been reported."

The screen shows grainy footage of the ship being guided in by another boat as the newscaster discusses the tragedies like it's any other day.

I scrambled off the ground, calling Connie.

"Hey, sweet girl."

"Have you seen the news?" My voice comes out breathy, like I've been running for hours.

"It's not them." Her reply is automatic, like she was waiting for me to call.

"You're sure?"

She lets out a long sigh. "Yeah, I know where they are. Hayes gave me the code. Do you want to know?"

I shake my head, even though she can't see it. I don't want to know. I don't want to obsess over everything happening in that country. Wondering where they are is one thing; knowing where they are is completely another. It's better for my sanity to not have that information. *Says the one watching the news all the time, like she's seventy-five and not twenty-one.*

"No, thanks, though. Just keep me updated if anything happens."

"I'm sorry, Charlie. I love you. Things will get better, I promise." Connie has always been nonpareil, and this is no different. She listened to everything I told her about the Carter situation, and she didn't doubt me once.

Sighing, I end the call and decide to take a shower. My good mood has been ruined, and I'm falling back into my normal depressed state.

I turn the water scalding hot, hoping it'll burn off the tension and anxiety that have built up inside me. As the steam fills the bathroom, I try to focus on the soothing sensation of the water against my skin and not my thoughts of Hayes. It doesn't work though, he's always on the forefront of my mind. It's depressing how much I miss him, miss his voice, miss his smell. Simply thinking about him and I swear I can smell peppermint. I continue to stand in the water until it starts to turn cold.

Moving the flimsy shower curtain out of my way, I reach for my towel on the hook without taking my eyes off the ground. I feel exhausted; the highs and lows of today have taken a toll on me. The weight of my emotions feels unbearable as I wrap the towel around myself.

"Charlotte."

My blood runs as cold as the water I was just standing under. The pompous voice sends shivers down my spine as my attention snaps up to the intruder.

Carter is standing in my bathroom doorway.

"What are you doing here?" I shriek at him.

His chin tips to the side as he looks at me, mystified. "We need to talk."

I stare at him, my mouth gaping open. He looks unhinged, like he hasn't slept in days. His hair is disheveled and greasy, and his clothes are dingy like he's been wearing them for days or even longer. From hot surfer to sloppy stoner.

"You need to leave." I try to keep my voice steady and be assertive, but the shake is undeniable.

He holds something up between two of his fingers, his eyes narrowing at me like I should know what it is. I glance between his hand and his eyes several times before I realize what he's holding. Uncle Roger's mint tin.

My voice comes out breathy as I try to make sense of what's going on. "How do you have that?"

"Mind telling me why *he* was here? Why he left *this* here? On our special night?!"

"What the fuck are you talking about?" I shriek at him.

"Now, now, Charlotte." He says through a condescending smirk while tapping the tin box on the bathroom counter. "Come on. I see how you look at me. You're my rose." I don't have time to process what he's saying before he pounces on me. He grabs the back of my neck while slamming his mouth into mine.

My towel instantly falls as I try to shove him away. He

doesn't realize it, but his vice-like grip around my neck automatically triggers my body into fight mode.

I raise my knee, slamming it into his groin before shoving him back.

He staggers backward but doesn't fall, so I start attacking with vengeance. Releasing weeks of anger, sadness, and fear onto him. I punch with everything I have in me, not taking any mercy as he tries to block my advances.

Thank God for my dad and Uncle Roger making me do years of self-defense and boxing classes. I haven't been in a little while, but the muscle memory kicks in and my body moves on instinct. Every punch and kick is calculated and aimed at vulnerable spots.

I can hear Uncle Roger in a loop saying, "Don't back down from sharks, Char. Don't back down, Charlotte! You kick his ass." Before, he was saying it in jest when referring to my sparring with one of the boys. Right now, I'm using it to fuel my rage.

So, I hit him with everything I have in me. Punch after punch, landing like he's my own boxing bag. Finally, I throw a left jab into his kidney and then a right punch directly into his jaw.

He unceremoniously falls backwards, eyes closed. *A knockout.*

I don't even take a second to admire the damage I've done. Or grab a towel. I simply skirt around him and run out my front door, screaming for someone to call 911.

The neighbor across from me is standing in her doorway, groceries in hand, still in her scrubs.

"Get in here!" She waves me into her apartment, slams the door, and locks it.

"Honey, take this! I'll get you clothes." She hands me her phone, already calling 911.

"911, what's your emergency?"

"I was just attacked in my apartment. Palmetto Commons #138."

"Do you need medical care?" The dispatcher asks.

"No. But he does."

I'm faintly aware of my neighbor draping a robe around me, but I haven't stopped looking through the peephole in her door. Making sure Carter doesn't leave. I don't know what I'll do if he tries to come through, but I'm preparing myself for another round of kicking-ass.

The police arrived within three minutes, and thankfully, he's still passed out on my bathroom floor.

The deputies hit me with a flood of questions and it took all of me to answer them calmly. It felt like the first night all over again, and I wanted to scream.

"No, he doesn't have a key."

"No, I don't know how he got in."

"Yes, I'm sure the door was locked."

"No, I didn't flirt with him or lead him on, you fucking asshole." I may have left the asshole part out, but I shouldn't have.

This time, I watched them haul him into an ambulance and cuff him to the gurney. His face was already beginning to swell and turn color.

Closing my eyes, I say a silent prayer of thanks to Uncle Roger and my dad. I know they'd be proud of me for that one.

Chapter Thirteen

Charlie

I damn near laughed in the officer's face when he told me my apartment was safe to go back into. *Again.*

My sweet neighbor helped me pack everything we could into my car. She didn't ask too many questions, just started putting things into bags and giving me reassuring looks. Despite the awful circumstances, her nurturing soul reminds me so much of my mom and Connie that I immediately felt comfortable around her. In the midst of it all, I didn't even ask her name, but I'll never forget all she has done for me today.

Once we had all the things I cared about in my car, I told her to keep or sell anything she wanted. If not, the property management could deal with it.

I'm never coming back to this apartment again.

I showed up at Connie's, in the middle of the night, with my car full of stuff and an exhausted heart. I hadn't called to tell her about the attack this time; problem-solving mode had kicked in and I worked on auto-pilot loading up my car.

She met me at the front door with a worried look on her

face. The alarm and camera must have alerted her when I pulled in. Hayes and Drew installed a state of the art system for her, even adding upgrades. She would've known I was here before the gate started opening.

"Charlotte Amelia Reynolds! What are you doing here so late?"

The sobs broke out of me at the sight of her and the concern in her voice. I'd been numb since the attack. Now that I'm safe and the adrenaline has worn off, though, I let it all out.

I fell into Connie, allowing her to hold me up.

She half carries me into the house as I stumble over my own feet. When she closes the door, I freeze and, through tears and hiccups, say, "Lock. Set. Alarm."

Frantically turning around, she throws the deadbolt into place and jams at the buttons on her alarm system. She looks as freaked out as I feel.

"Come on, sweet girl." I follow her to the couch and sit as close to her as I can. She puts her arms around my shoulders, allowing me to sink into her embrace.

"H-he. W-Was in. A-apartment." My chest heaves as I try to get the story out, but I can barely talk.

"Who was? Carter?"

"I, shower. Came in. Grabbed. Fought off. Neighbor police."

"Slow down, Charlie. Breathe for me, baby." I try to follow her lead, but I can't stop shaking. Everything is hitting me at once. Hayes leaving me and then Carter breaking into my apartment *again*.

Connie runs her fingers through my hair as she holds me. It takes a long time before my breathing evens to a steady rhythm, but she never let's go of me.

My voice sounds raspy as I finally start talking again.

"I got off the phone with you and went to take a shower. When I was getting out, he was standing in the bathroom. He *lunged* at me."

"No." Her fingers freeze in my hair, and it feels like she holds her breath.

"Do you remember when dad and Uncle Roger made me spar with the boys?"

She nods, and her lips let out a puff of air. "Your momma hated how hard they were on you."

A humorless chuckle falls out. "When Carter came at me, it was like Uncle Roger was in that bathroom telling me what to do. I just attacked."

Tears drip down her face, but a real smile comes out: "You were just a little girl back then. He wanted you to know how to defend yourself." My dad's approach was always a little softer, but Uncle Roger was the best kind of tough love. Encouraging but he never let me use being a girl as an excuse.

"Well, it worked. I knocked him out and ran out the door, naked."

Her eyebrows rose, and at the same time, her eyes widened. "Naked?"

Laughing with slight disbelief, even at myself, I explain. "When he grabbed me, my towel fell. I was too focused on 'neutralizing the threat' and then I wasn't going to waste time grabbing a towel while he was lying on the floor."

"Oh my. What happened after?"

"My neighbor was walking into her apartment, and when I ran out, she brought me into her place. I called 911, and she gave me something to cover up with. He was still on the floor when they got there. They arrested him."

Connie lets out a heavy sigh of relief and pats my shoulder. "You did so well. Your daddy and uncle would have been proud of you. Your mom, too."

Tears fill my eyes again, threatening to spill over.

"I packed up my apartment. My neighbor stayed with me the entire time and helped. I can't go back." I pause and take a look around. Everything about this house is filled with reminders of Hayes. "And I can't stay here."

She pulls back from me. "And why can't you stay here?"

A million "becauses" roll through my brain. Because this is Hayes' safe place. Because he was my safe place. Because he hates me. Because my heart is broken. Because everywhere around here, all I see is him.

I need time to heal without being held back by the past.

And if I'm a little honest with myself, I'm scared.

"Finals are done. I'm a college graduate, and my plan was always to go to Hayes. Now that we aren't together—"

She interrupts me, not being able to contain her feelings. "That boy. I'm so mad at him."

"Don't be. He overreacted, but I can't say I wouldn't have done the same had I seen a girl in his bed. Especially with all the stress he's going through." That moment has run through my head a thousand times. I knew Hayes was struggling with nerves and us being apart. I hadn't realized how bad it had gotten, but all of it mixing together just created one big toxic mess.

"He's going to overreact when he hears this." She grumbles out.

"No! You can't tell him or Drew! Not until they get home. They won't do anything but worry themselves sick and take responsibility. They need to focus on what they're doing." I can't be the distraction that doesn't bring one of them home. The deployments aren't easy for them, even without all this added on. It's life or death for them every day, sometimes. If they're distracted for a moment, it could be the end for them.

Connies eyes fill with sympathy as she nods her head. "I

don't know if I agree with keeping it from them, but it's not my story to tell."

"Thank you." I settled back on the couch.

"Back to where you plan on going."

"I don't know." I tell her honestly. "I just need to go. I have some money saved up and a good car. Odessa mentioned she would be in Seattle at the end of the summer. The plan starts forming the more I talk. I can take a little road trip and go visit Odessa and see a little bit more of the country on my way.

"You're more like your mother than you think. She was always about the next adventure. Every one of our family vacations was planned by her and her sense of adventure." She smiles warmly, reminiscing about her late, best friend.

"I think it will be good for me to spread my wings a bit."

"You'll call? Send your location?"

My eyes close as I cringe. "I can't. I don't know when Carter will get out, and I don't want anyone to know where I am.

"Charlotte." Her frown deepens as she takes in my answer.

I hold my hand up, trying to think of something quickly. "I'm sure we can find an app to call from that doesn't track location."

If Connie didn't live in a double-gated community and carry a gun with her everywhere, I would be concerned about her as well. I know she can handle herself, though, and she has neighbors all around her who watch out for her. As well as the security system.

It's me that Carter has a weird obsession with anyway.

She's looking at me like she's about to protest, but when she sees how serious I am, she relents. "You call once a month and text more. If you miss even one call, I will tell your brother *and* Hayes."

I nod my head in agreement. "I can do that."

"When are you leaving?"

"I'll stay a day or two. I need to go to sleep and talk to the detective. Get a new phone and number. Pull out as much cash as I can."

"Put it on prepaid VISAs. I don't want you traveling with only cash. You can get the cash and put it on gift cards or a prepaid visa. There's Target and Walmart everywhere."

I glance at Connie with a newfound respect. "You planning on running away, too?"

Her laugh brings lightness to my dark mood. "Roge always had a getaway plan. But I don't want you to stay at any cash-only motels. How about the motorhome?"

I blink at her, trying to tell if she's kidding or not.

She wants me to take her motorhome. Across the country.

It's a smaller Class C but it has all the bells and whistles. I don't know exactly how much it is worth, but I guarantee it's worth more than the average starter home in South Carolina. She uses it nearly every weekend during the summer, when she and her friends go camping. Now, she's offering it up like it's a t-shirt to borrow.

"Are you serious?"

She nods and grins. "I trust you'll take good care of it. You've always been brave, sweet girl. I don't want what this man did or Hayes leaving to stomp out any of that fearlessness. I've always wanted the two of you to be together. However, I don't like the way he handled the situation that night. I love that boy, but he should've treated you with more respect. I know how long you two have been pining for each other but maybe it's time you found yourself beyond Hayes. Take some time to figure out who Charlie is. What *she* really wants."

Her words hit me hard, but she's right. I've been caught up in being Hayes' girlfriend, giving every ounce of free time to him and our future. Even before we were together, he was part of all of my decisions. Don't get me wrong; I loved that. I'd still choose that time and time again. But now I need to pivot. I need to focus on myself, what I want, and where I want to be. Follow in Odessa's footsteps a little more and pave my own way. Maybe Hayes and I will work it out, or maybe we won't. Either way, I shouldn't waste anymore time dwelling on what could have been.

Chapter Fourteen

Charlie

Thursday, June 1.

Leaving Connie's house was bittersweet to say the least. I was beyond sad to leave Connie, but still a little excited to have a plan and get away from South Carolina. We celebrated my next chapter with a bottle of wine and a movie night. Nothing too crazy, considering I planned on leaving first thing this morning.

The motorhome was ready, Connie had gone over everything twice, and I had a cheat sheet written down with instructions. I tried to assure her that I could Google whatever I needed to, but Connie insisted that I have it on paper. I saw the worry on her face only growing stronger the closer it got to me leaving, but she never tried to convince me to stay.

I pulled out of the driveway right at dawn, with a passenger seat full of snacks that Connie had packed next to my purse that now holds Hayes' mint tin. My neighbor must have found it while we were packing up my apartment and placed it in there without me knowing. I tried to convince Connie to keep it or send it to Hayes but she refused. She said I needed the "good-luck" on my new adventure and she wouldn't be able to get his address anyway.

The second I hit the interstate, time started to blend together. I thought that I would take my time sight-seeing, but I couldn't bring myself to stop. My excitement quickly dwindled as the fear of being alone overtook me.

The only time I felt safe was when I was driving. I made sure to find the nicest RV parks and then time it so that I would pull in an hour before sunset. I'd eat, try to sleep, and wake up before the sun even began to rise again. Once those first rays began lighting up the sky, I was on the road. Stopping only for gas and food, I set my eyes on the Pacific. Needing to get as far away as possible, as quickly as possible. After that, I'll reassess.

I just drove and drove.

Drove until I was across the country.

It wasn't until I hit the Idaho/Oregon border that it felt like I could breathe again.

The landscape quickly became some of the most beautiful I'd seen on the entire trip. Or maybe I was just slowing down enough to pay attention. Tall cliffs and a lush green landscape surrounded the winding river as I drove alongside it. Wild-flowers were just starting to bloom, adding bursts of color in every direction.

Then I drove through wide, open hay fields where it felt like you could see for miles. It was as if I were driving through an old western film. My dad would have loved it. Drew and I watched more John Wayne movies than anything else with him. I could feel the nostalgia starting to unravel the knot of anxiety I had developed.

I didn't stop to admire the large town I saw next; didn't even look at the name. My eyes were only set on the mountains I saw in the distance. It felt like they were calling to me. Every mile that I got closer to them, my body relaxed. When I hit the edge of a small town, Three Sisters, OR, every part of me begged to get out and walk down the bustling of Main Street. To explore as if I was one of the other carefree tourists. A quick Google search sent me in the direction of a quaint RV park. The reviews looked phenomenal, but the pictures hadn't done its justice. Nestled between the pine trees and Cascade mountains, sat my own little hideout.

The check-in area of the RV park is a cabin that has a front desk, a sitting area, and a small coffee station. It's nothing fancy, but the cowboy chic decor is fitting and welcoming. The woman behind the counter has big, teased blonde '80's hair and a huge grin.

"Hello! Welcome to the Cascadia RV Park and lodging. You checkin' in?" Her accent doesn't sound Southern, but there is a distinct twang to it.

"I am, but I don't have a reservation." I try to smile, but my face feels stiff from the last few days of clenching my teeth.

She grins back, like she's unfazed by my lack of expression. "No worries, doll face. How many nights are you staying?"

"Just one for now." I'm not sure how long I'll feel comfortable here. For all I know, this could be a fluke and I'll be having a panic attack in the next ten minutes.

"Okay, if you want to add more, just let me or Roger know."

My head snaps up. "Roger?"

"My husband. He's always around here somewhere."

I nod and a small smile forms at the corner of my lips. I love that there's another Roger around here somewhere.

I glance at her name tag to thank her and my breath feels like it was stolen right from my chest. Her name is Jessie, the same as my dad's, only spelled slightly differently.

I don't normally believe in signs but I can't deny there's something in the universe telling me this is the place to be.

I swallow down the emotions but my eyes definitely feel a little misty. "Perfect. Thank you so much. Is there anywhere you recommend for dinner?"

"Definitely the SnowPeak diner; it's on Main Street, right in the middle of town. Best milkshakes you've ever had and the burgers aren't bad either. There's a path that you can use to walk there if you feel like stretching your legs."

I nod and smile, not able to say anything else. Without realizing it, she just handed me the third sign that I belong here. Anytime we would have a bad day, my dad would say, "There's no problem a burger and a shake can't fix, and if it can't fix it, at least you had a burger and a shake." Sage words of wisdom to any small child, but it was always our thing. Lost a game? Burger and a milkshake. Bad grade? Burger and a milkshake. Mom's pissed because we forgot to thaw the frozen chicken, like she asked? Burger and a milkshake.

After I parked the motor home, I took a little extra time getting everything set up. It's hot outside, but the dry heat feels good on my skin after three days of sitting in air conditioning. Taking Jessie's advice, I decided to walk the trail. I took my time, enjoying the much needed serenity that Central Oregon was bringing me.

I expected to feel the same unsafe feeling I've been having once I got into town but it never came. The town itself oozes charm; the buildings look like they were built a hundred years ago but are well taken care of. People continued to stroll down the sidewalks, smiling and having a good time. It wasn't that I was ignored, but no one seemed to look at me longer than to offer a friendly smile.

The small diner was busy but I was lucky enough to get a table off to the side. The waitress took my order in a rush, smiling and assuring me it'd be right out. I got a little lost watching her work. The system she had to manage the rush was memorizing. Every customer looked happy as she glided from table to table, delivering food. All of the locals greeted each other and all of the tourists settled in as if they were home.

For the first time since the Carter incident, I looked around a crowded room and felt safe.

I may actually stick around.

Chapter Fifteen

Charlie

The next morning, I woke up later than I had in weeks. My body's natural response to this place had me crashing hard and sleeping harder. So hard, there was drool pooling on my pillow.

I decided last night that I wanted to stay an extra day or two and just meander through the town. On my walk last night, I looked through the windows of the local stores and fell in love with the art and gift shops. Today, I'm allowing myself to explore and see what else is around. See if last night was a fever dream or if this place really does have a little healing power.

As soon as I got back into town, the uniqueness that drew me in yesterday hit me again. Traffic slows as cars drive down Main Street, but it doesn't seem as if anyone is in a hurry. Locals and tourists vibe with such ease that I can't tell which is which. It's a Thursday, but it seems like every day is a weekend here. *I freaking love it.*

The first store I went into was a clothing store that only sold alpaca apparel. Everything was made from alpaca wool—socks, gloves, jackets, and blankets. All things made locally by the owner and her family. I spent nearly an hour talking to Camila, the owner's daughter, about their farm and why her parents ended up settling in Oregon. If I wasn't 'ballin' on a budget' and summer wasn't right around the corner, I could've bought the entire store. Instead, I left with a pair of hiking socks and the potential of a new friend.

Out of my peripheral vision, I look up just in time to see an older woman step off the curb. I watch in what feels like slow motion as her foot goes one way and her body goes the other. Within a blink, she's falling into the road.

I immediately sprint to her side and crouch down in front of her. "Ma'am! Ma'am, are you okay?"

Before she answers, I quickly look around our surroundings to make sure there aren't any cars coming. Luckily, this is a side street and it's empty. The last thing we need is to be hit by a car that doesn't see us.

She gingerly tries to roll to her side and holds her wrist for support while groaning. "Oh, sweet heavens." Her wrist is already swelling and turning colors.

I stand up and look around just as a police officer starts driving by on Main Street. Without thinking, I move into action. Throwing my hands in the air, I practically jump in front of the moving vehicle. It isn't going fast enough to cause any real damage if it hits me, but in hindsight, probably not my safest idea.

The officer slams on his breaks and throws his hands in the air, looking at me incredulously.

When he gets out, the sight of him almost takes my breath away. He looks like Captain America meets an angry Ken Doll. Tall, blonde, and blue-eyed with perfect straight white teeth.

"What are you doing?" His tone isn't angry but it's definitely not happy either. Then again, I just threw myself in front of his moving vehicle.

"I am so sorry, sir! This woman just fell and I think she needs medical attention." I point toward the woman, who is still barely able to support herself.

He glances over, now noticing the fallen woman. "Elise! You okay?"

She shakes her head but says, "I'll be fine, Danny."

Instead of standing there any longer, I move back to my original spot kneeling in front of her as he radio's something in.

I talk to her softly, like I would if she were my own grand-mother. "Ma'am, we really should have a professional check you over. You took quite a fall. Can I call someone for you?"

"Don't you worry, honey. I'm sure ole Sergeant Turner is already calling my husband Cal *and* the rest of the town." She gives him a stern look, and he smirks in response.

Walking over to us, he says, "Let's get you out of the road, and then I'll make those calls."

He grips under her waist and I grab the elbow of the unin-jured arm, hoping to help balance. She limps a little while holding her wrist close to her chest. As soon as she's sitting on the bench, my body relaxes a fraction.

"Mind if I sit with you while we wait?" I ask, not quite ready to leave her alone. It seems like she knows Sergeant Turner but I still don't feel comfortable just leaving her.

She smiles at me and the corners of her eyes crease. "I'd love that, darling. Just stopping through town?"

I swallowed a lump of emotion that came out of nowhere and nodded.

"Where ya from, sweetie?"

"A small town in South Carolina, Heartsville."

"I figured somewhere in the south. You beautiful southern belles have such charm."

I choke on a laugh and look at my worn-out baby blue Vans

and jeans. Not many people back home would refer to me as a southern belle; definitely no debutants or tea parties for me.

"Thank you. How's your wrist? And ankle? Does anything else hurt?"

"I'll be just fine. These old bones bruise easily."

An ambulance pulls up and out of the passenger seat, pops out an identical version of the sergeant. My jaw truly drops when I see him. How on earth this town has two men that look like this is beyond me.

"Daniel Turner!" Elise begins to scold him. "You went and called the medics?!"

The medic in question walked up with a lopsided grin full of playfulness. "Elise, my love. You know, it's only the best for you."

"You telling me *you're* the best they got, Levi?" She arches her eyebrow and purses her lips. "Where's Brian? Or Bill?"

He grabs at his chest dramatically, and I can't help the giggle that escapes. It feels like it's been months since I've laughed.

"I'm insulted that you think those imbeciles are better than me!" He crouches down in front of the bench and opens up his medic bag, pulling out a blood pressure cuff.

Before he places it on her, he glances at me and then does a double take. His eyes roam my face, and his flirty smile lets me know he likes the view. "You must be the hero that jumped in front of a moving cruiser."

Sergeant Turner appears behind him and grips his shoulder, lovingly chastising him. "Focus on your job, Vi."

Levi chuckles and gets back to work. The resemblance between them is uncanny. If they weren't wearing different uniforms, there's no way I'd be able to tell which twin was which.

I look at Elise, who is grinning at me like she knows exactly what I'm thinking.

"Does everyone in town look like this?"

Her lips twitch as she looks between the two of them. "No, but the Turner genes are impenetrable. Their daddy looked just like they did at this age, and Dan's son Ben is a tiny mini-me as well."

Levi shrugs. "It's the best. I get to share my genetics without having to settle down. I'm Levi, by the way, and the replica behind me is Dan."

Dan rolls his eyes. "I heard you tell Elise you're just visiting. How long you staying for?"

I puff out my cheeks as I let out a breath. "I'm not sure. I don't really have any place to be for a little while."

His eyes narrow as he takes in the subtle undertones of what I'm not saying. "You in some sort of trouble?"

I let out one humorless laugh. "No, nothing like that. I just graduated from the University of South Carolina. I thought a road trip might help me clear my head and figure out my next steps." I don't know why I'm opening up so much to these people I've never met before, but I can't stop the words coming out of my mouth. *Maybe spending so many days alone in the car has me desperate for human interaction.*

Dan's eyebrows furrow in concern. "But you don't have a plan? Find a job or settle down somewhere?"

I shrug, feeling a mix of uncertainty and freedom. "I guess I'll figure it out along the way. Right now, I just need some time to explore. Find myself, again."

He nods slowly, and his lips twist to the side. "My wife, albeit a real-life superhero, is feeling a touch overwhelmed with running a company and being an amazing mother. If you decide to stay around, even if only a couple weeks, I'm sure she could use the help."

I give him a polite smile, still unsure of my timeline. "Thank you. I appreciate the offer."

"She owns the Cascades Property Management company here in town. Two blocks that way," he gestures to the south of where we are standing. "She's renovating the inside, so it may be a little chaotic right now."

"Another reason we need you. I mean, *she* needs you." Levi says, and then winks.

An older gentleman comes running from the other side of the road, yelling, "Lise!"

She smiles and hollers, "I'm fine, Cal! Levi here got me all checked out!"

Levi stands and pats the newcomer's shoulder. "She's okay, but I think she should have a doc look at that wrist and ankle. Make sure nothing is broken."

Cal looks at me with a warm smile and says, "Thank you for rescuing my heart. I didn't catch your name."

Tears threaten to fill my eyes at his sweet words. You can tell he loves his wife more than anything.

I end up introducing myself as Charlie, forgetting that I should probably use a fake name.

When I look over at Dan, he's standing by his cruiser on the phone. When he hangs up, he shouts, "My wife's name is Olivia. She'll be expecting you." Then he gives me one nod and slides into the front seat, smiling.

I walk the two blocks south, still not even sure if I want to go into the building. A large sign is out front with pretty writing, "Cascades Property Management."

I try to open the door, but it's locked, so I knock quietly. Half-hoping no one would answer.

I didn't expect a dark-haired woman with her brown hair in a bun, wearing yoga pants, and an oversized shirt to open the door. After seeing Dan, I expected a very put together housewife to be on the other side. Olivia, however, looks like every other mom in the trenches of motherhood. She can't be much older than I am, but our lives are on completely different routes.

She opens the door with a toddler attached to her hip. Elise was right; this little boy is the spitting image of his dad.

"It's so nice to meet you! I'm Olivia and this is Ben." She greets me as Ben tucks his head into her neck while smiling shyly at me. He can't be much older than three.

"Hi! I heard you need me." I say, trying to muster up as much courage and confidence as I can.

She grins back at me and motions for me to follow her inside. "I need an army right now. I just found out I'm pregnant and I'm drowning in bookwork and potty training."

We make small talk as she shows me around the building. Asking where I'm from and what my degree is. I try to keep everything light and positive while explaining my history but every question she asks has me word vomiting more and more of my story.

The building is empty except for one lone desk in the corner of the first floor. The bones are good, though, so Olivia gets to start with a blank slate.

A staircase leads to the second floor, which is in the middle of the room. I widen my eyes at the sheer grandiosity of this space. It's huge up here—completely open and bare.

"What do you have planned for up here?" I ask with genuine curiosity.

She lets out a tired sigh. "The contractor will be here next week to put up glass partitions. I'm going for an industrial vibe that separates work and play. I'll still be able to see the kids playing so I can get work done but I need things to be separated. Two offices parallel to each other, a full kitchen, and a playroom. Besides the crew that I have to take care of the properties and my accountant, it's just me running the business. My adopted mother, Lovey, left everything to me a few years ago. I've been trying to keep the same standards she had, grow the business, and also raise Ben—all while being a good wife. It's been a surprisingly big undertaking. In case you can't tell by the outfit."

I nod and give her a reassuring smile. She's got more on her plate than most but she just keeps smiling.

"Well, I'd be happy to help. Whether that be with Ben so you can get stuff done or whatever you delegate to me, the only thing is that I'm not sure how long I'll be here. And..." I chew on the edge of my nail while I try to think of the right way to explain my circumstances. I don't know how to tell her I can't be traced without sounding like a crazy person running from the law.

"I don't want anyone to know that I'm here."

Her head tilts to the side for a second and then she nods. "Let's go get something to eat and talk about details."

We walk down to the SnowPeak and I order the same thing as yesterday: a burger and a milkshake.

"Do you feel comfortable telling me what you are running from? I promise you, I'm a vault. Even my husband doesn't need to know everything." She gives me a reassuring look that says no matter what, she has my back.

My shoulders sag as I contemplate telling her everything. I don't know if Carter is still in jail or if he's on house arrest, like the detective assigned to the case said he might be. The threat of him finding me still feels real, but other than myself, I don't necessarily have anything to hide. Olivia feels like a safe person that I can vent to, and I could really use a friend right now.

The more I talk, the more I end up spilling though. Until my entire story is thrown out on the table in front of us. From Hayes, to Carter in my bed, to the attack, to leaving South Carolina.

I'm sure that I end up talking about Hayes more than anything. He's been at the forefront of my mind, even despite the attack. The most hurt I've felt comes from him. He was always such a protector in my life and for him to abandon me like that rocked me to the core. Now I'm stuck in limbo until he gets back and can be reasoned with. If he even will at all.

She listens intently and then shakes her head with a small grin, tugging the corner of her lip up. "That man is going to beat himself up when he finds out." She has no idea how much. Hayes has always been the worrier, trying to fix everything. This situation may set him over the edge, but right now he isn't my problem. He's focused on his career and staying alive. I'm focused on figuring out my own life.

"I'd like to hire you as my assistant. Under the table. Cash. There's no expectations, and when you're ready to leave... Well, I have a feeling I'll miss you, but I'll understand."

Relief washes through me. I could use the money, and the fact she's taking a chance on me seems like a once-in-a million opportunity.

Tears well in my eyes as I say, "Thank you, Olivia."

With a laugh, she says, "Don't thank me yet. You have no idea how far behind I've gotten."

Chapter Sixteen

Hayes

Friday, September 29.

Surviving hell isn't easy but when you realize you don't have much to lose anymore, it gets surprisingly easier. I'm not worried about getting home to Charlie or starting our family. My only focus is right here, right now. Let the bullets fly and the bad guys die.

That's what this place is, though: hell. There's no shortage of carnage and gunfire around the crumbling city. A true war zone. Black smoke fills the air from tire fires, shots echo off the buildings, bodies lay haphazardly on the ground. It feels like I'm living in a video game. The numbness to death around has enveloped us all.

However, I wouldn't choose to be anywhere else. Mothers and their children have been ripped from their homes, murdered or even worse raped and left on the side of the road to die. Fathers forced to watch and then tortured to death. The enemy has no rules, no morals, no care for human life. If we can offer any form of protection, any sense of help, that's all that matters. Even if it means risking our lives to do it.

It wasn't long before the fear of dying evaporated and, left in its place, was a "fuck-it" attitude. We're doing what we've been training to do: kill for the greater good.

We've been inching our way back in, trying to take the city back. Peeking out through small holes in the buildings with our rifles, watching for any sign of the enemy.

"Woah, holy shit." Keller announced to me and the three other guys hiding out in the abandoned elementary school. Drew, Lincoln, and my head snap up at once to see where he has his sights on. We joke that Keller's too pretty to be a SEAL but the man may be the finest sniper I know. It's not his fault that he looks like he belongs in one of the rom-coms that Everett's obsessed with but it's the only thing we can truly mess with him about.

"No gun, but it isn't the 90's. Why the fuck he got a walkie-talkie? Everyone around here uses cell phones."

My sight lines up with the military-aged man that Keller spotted. He's clearly relaying information while he's looking toward the front lines of the fighting that's happening just to the north of him. Our team isn't directly involved in the fight, but our objective is still to protect the Iraqi military and the US soldiers helping them.

We all studied the man, watching for even one more sign of ill intent. Everything about him has our spider senses tingling. From his posture to the way he's reporting on the walkie-talkie.

Lincoln notices the four men sitting in the room adjacent to the balcony at the same time I do. We can clearly see the men loading up bags full of weapons. "Take the shot."

Keller doesn't even think twice; he shoots and the man falls to the ground. The men in the room immediately stand and we notice more guns. Radioing and shouting start to ensue between the four. A group of at least seven other men appear in the building to the south of them and we all realize that we are going to have to start covering a lot more ground to keep our guys protected.

Shots in our direction start ringing out and I don't even bat an eye. The sights on my rifle stay trained on the building and we all start picking guys off one by one.

One man is left, laying low, hiding. I'm so focused on watching that window, waiting for a glimpse of him to show that I barely register the shouts happening around me. I roll my body to the side, just as an RPG round blasts through the window on the far side of the room we are in.

Mother fucker.

The room shakes, as shrapnel flies. The curse words start flowing through the room as everyone scrambles to get our shit and get out of here. Not only do we have a target on our backs but this room is completely unstable. Five seconds later and another one hits the same spot as the first.

Smoke and debris fill the air, but it doesn't impact our routine. Everyone stays low, moving quickly and efficiently.

It isn't until I'm almost completely packed that I notice the blood covering the floor. I do a quick glance over myself and then look out at the room. Keller and Drew are shoving gear into their packs as fast as they can. Lincoln sits against the far wall, radioing in for backup.

"Who's hit!" I growl out, nearly shouting at them.

Drew and Keller both look to me, then to the blood on the floor, then at each other.

Lincoln makes eye contact with me, then down at his leg. I zero on the blood soaking through the left side of his torn pants. He's still giving off coordinates and instructions like he isn't bleeding out all over the floor.

My body's automatic response is anger. A new hit of adrenaline pumps through my body. The chutzpah he has to not let us know he's been hit has me ready to rage.

I march over with my med bag, so that I can get a better look. I'm not the medic on our team and it's been a while since that was my role, but I at least have the training. Drew takes the radio from Lincoln, shaking his head. He's clearly as pissed as I am, but neither of us call him out on it.

The wound on the side of his upper thigh is pouring blood like someone turned on a faucet. His entire body is already turning a dangerous shade of white from the blood loss.

"You're not going to like this." He needs a tourniquet and surgery. Which means he's getting a med-evac out of here, no matter what.

"Just fucking do it." His normal gruff tone sounds hollow. I can guarantee if it weren't for the adrenaline still coursing through his veins, he'd have passed out already.

Unzipping the small med bag that I never leave without, I pull out the tourniquet and get to work as fast as I can. Trying to treat a nightmare of a wound in a nightmare of a situation. At this point, I don't even know if his leg will be salvageable by the time he gets to the operating room or if he will even make it there. I don't have time to dwell on it though, Linc's evac is about to arrive. Guns blazing.

I throw Lincoln over my shoulder as Drew and Keller take point to cover us. We've got a dark narrow hallway to get down, and then once we are out we need to get to the back of the building. The only problem being we will be completely exposed the second that door opens. We have to plan it just right so that the Apache we called in can be our distraction. It'll rain hellfire like no other to clear the way for the Black Hawk.

We all move in sync, letting our muscle memory take over. The door stays closed as we wait for the signal.

"Party in ten, gentleman." Comes through and I almost grin.

That guy is saving our ass and he sounds a whole hell of a lot like Everett. I don't know if it's him, but I guarantee we'll never hear the end of it, if it was.

On cue, ten seconds later we hear the signature sound of laser-guided hellfire missiles hitting the coordinates we called in. Drew opens the door, nods and we all file through. Sticking close to the side of the building as we make our way around it.

Within thirty seconds, we hear the familiar buzz of a Black Hawk. It doesn't even land, just hovers as two men start propelling down.

I gently set him down and then squeeze his shoulder. His eyes are open and staring at me but the way his lips are quivering tells me even he knows how bad this is.

"Don't you dare give up, Linc. You see that light you turn the fuck around." I know he can't hear me, but it needs to be said. "See ya soon, brother."

With a nod, I back away and let the medics do what they need to. Once he's safely in the bird, I watch as it flies away. It takes no time at all before it's gotten the hell out of here as fast as it could.

I make eye contact with Drew. A silent conversation about how messed up this entire situation passes between us.

Keller starts giving commands, and we both start moving again.

Back to the shitshow that has become our life.

Happy fucking birthday to me.

Chapter Seventeen

Charlie

Monday, November 27.

The next several months passed in a blur. Olivia wasn't exaggerating when she said she was overwhelmed and behind. After seeing how much she's been doing alone, I'm shocked it wasn't worse. She's running a multi-million-dollar company by herself and as much as I love Dan, he's solely focused on his career right now. I haven't minded the challenges it's all brought, though. It's kept me plenty busy—a respite from everything that happened in South Carolina.

I drove the motorhome back to Heartsville a few weeks ago. The detective on the case, Detective Paul, thought that it was important that I be at the trial and give my victim impact speech. Carter never stopped looking at me—the obsession still lurking under that creepy smile. The way he watched me even had Detective Paul on edge, so I left immediately after I gave my statement. To my relief, Connie stayed and was the one to tell me he would be going to prison.

Evidently, I wasn't the first of Carter's victims. When he

was a minor, he was stalking a girl he went to high school with. Because of his age and social standing, he barely received a slap on the wrist. This time, though, he wasn't so lucky. The same judge who presided over his original case, Judge Shapiro, was appointed to this case. Not only did she remember him, she was determined to ensure justice was served this time around. Carter received the maximum sentence—five years— and was ordered to undergo mandatory counseling for his behavior.

I was on a flight out of there the day after the judge gave her ruling. Back to my new home. My safe place.

I'm not going to lie and say it hasn't been hard to readjust back to normal life, but it isn't as hard as I thought it would be. Especially now that the contractors have finally finished making our office building beautiful—if you can call a brick building beautiful. The second floor has the set-up of most people's dream home. The full kitchen itself is a masterpiece —I don't even like cooking but I might start just so I can use all the fancy equipment. The game room has a huge TV, bean bag chairs, and a Lego table that is bigger than my kitchen. Our actual "office" has views of the Cascade Mountains that take my breath away every time I look out the window.

Olivia and I have been exhausting ourselves the last few weeks, making sure we have everything we could ever need for the office and a new baby. Her due date is next week, but that hasn't stopped her from working. She walks up and down the stairs, carrying "light" boxes, claiming she's trying to induce labor. Meanwhile, it only worries Dan and me that she's overexerting herself. We both end up doing double the amount of work so that it's done faster and she will just sit. So far, it isn't working.

Finally, after an exhausting number of trips up the stairs, Dan couldn't handle it anymore. "Olivia! Please, baby, just stay up here and start organizing. We know that you can handle all of the work, but Charlie and I can't handle watching you do it."

Her eyes narrowed in response, looking fully pissed off.

I almost laugh every time I see her so angry. She's been like this for the last three weeks. Everything he says sets her off, and I can tell he's scrambling to appease her.

"I'm fine!" She growls out.

"Yes, you are!" I offer my insincere support. "Get things moving! That way, when it's time, you'll be so tired that they'll have to give you a c-section. Just lay back and let them do all the work." I shrug nonchalantly, knowing that's exactly what she doesn't want.

She huffs at me but takes a seat at her new desk. "Whatever."

I make eye contact with Dan and wink. His shoulders visibly relax, and he pinches the bridge of his nose. He's stressing himself out, watching her stress out.

<hr>

One a.m., and my phone starts ringing, startling me awake from a nightmare that Carter was in my bed again. Only this time, to add an extra layer of horror, it was my bed in Three Sisters. I don't have nightmares that often but when I do, my entire day is ruined. Shaking off the vivid dreams isn't an easy feat. Especially because the threat is still there. Someday, Carter will get out of prison and I highly doubt he isn't going to be looking for revenge, or even worse, still be obsessed with me.

I see Dan's name on the caller ID and immediately answer.

"Char, it's time. Pop is staying with Ben, and we are almost to the hospital. Olivia wants to know if you'll meet us there."

The emotion from the dream must still be coursing through

my veins because all of a sudden I'm crying as I throw my shoes and winter jacket over my pajamas while rushing out the door.

In such a short amount of time, the Turners have become my family. Inviting me to see the birth of their new child feels like the biggest blessing I've had in a long time. Since I first met them, really.

I made it to the hospital in Bend in record time, practically skidding into the parking lot. Levi follows suit, backing his behemoth of a truck in next to my car.

He jumps out, wearing sweatpants and a short-sleeve tee. Apparently, he was in the same rush that I was to get here. *At least I grabbed a jacket, though.*

He flings my door open and gasps in pretend shock. "Thought I was the only one invited to this shindig!"

"I can't believe you were even invited at all!"

He laughs, "Technically, I was invited to wait in the waiting room. Total B.S., if you ask me. I've delivered babies before, and I know how all the parts work." He hints suggestively.

I roll my eyes as we walk up to the hospital. "Yes, that's exactly what your sister-in-law wants to hear."

"Told her the same thing when Ben was born but she wouldn't let me in then either."

Levi greets the staff by first name as we walk through the sterile halls. Everyone here loves him, smiling and waving, congratulating him on being an uncle again. He's got a big heart, hidden beneath all that sass and sarcasm.

"Think you'll settle down? Maybe have kids someday?" He's a few years from thirty, but his brother has been married for almost five years.

He gives me that signature lopsided grin and wink. "You offering?"

Chuckling, I shut him down with ease. "You're too old for me."

"True and you're still wrapped up in that ex of yours." *Isn't that the truth?*

Levi's always been a flirt, but he flirts with everyone. He's like a golden retriever that wants to be loved, but the second he gets attention, he's on to the next. Almost like Everett. Matter of fact, that's probably why I like him so much. He's just easy to be around.

"To answer your question, though, probably not. I'll leave the marriage and babies to Dan. At least we know *he* won't fuck it up."

I almost get a chance to question him on what that means, but we get to labor and delivery and he takes a seat in the waiting room.

Knocking once, I open the door to Olivia's dark and quiet room.

She's bouncing on a large ball next to the bed and gritting her teeth. "Why the hell don't I want the drugs again?"

Dan places his head into his hands before groaning. "Don't answer that. It's a trick question."

Walking up to her, I gently put my hand on her shoulder. "You said that you want to have the most natural birth possible, but if that's changed, we can grab the doctor and get that needle jammed right into your spine."

She looks at me with horror in her eyes and then sighs. "No, I'll be fine." Right as she gets the last word out, a contraction hits, and she doubles over in pain. A slew of curse words that would put my brother and Hayes to shame are released from her. I glance at Dan, who looks both amused and terrified.

The nurse comes in, helping to guide Olivia back to the bed and check her dilation.

"It's time!" The nurse sings songs as she takes off the gloves that she just put on. "Let me grab the doctor and we can deliver this little girl."

Within fifteen minutes and a couple pushes, a tiny baby is placed into Olivia's arms.

Dan cuts the umbilical cord and I try to take several photos but honestly, they're probably blurry with how much I've cried.

"Want me to go tell Levi?"

Dan nods as he blinks away tears. "Thanks, Charlie."

I walk out to the waiting room with tears still streaming down my face. Seeing a dad so happy to welcome his baby girl into the world has me choked up. I can't help but think of my dad and how much I miss him. I've seen all the photos of my birth, and my dad looked the same way; starstruck and glowing with love and adoration. Of course, my thoughts also went to Hayes. Will he be this happy someday? Will it be me he's looking at like that, or another woman?

Levi jumps out of his chair when he sees me in a panic and I run into his arms. "They're okay! One healthy baby, and her mom did amazing!"

He squeezes his arms around my shoulders tighter before relaxing his shoulders and pulling back.

"What's with the crying, then?"

I fan my face and a sad laugh bubbles out. "It was just so sweet, ya know? Seeing Dan with this tiny baby and how proud he was of Olivia."

"Shit." He looks toward where I walked from. "I'm gonna cry too."

"Probably, you're even sappier than I am."

"Says the woman with snot running out of her nose." He grins back.

We both go back into the room after we've given them some

time with *Ellie.* Eleanor Anne Turner, to be exact. Levi coos at her and holds her like he's done it a thousand times. I don't know why he's so hell bent on thinking he wouldn't be a good dad, because he's a *really* great uncle.

Chapter Eighteen

Hayes

Saturday, May 26.

Thirteen months into a deployment that should have been only a year. The worst part is that we just found out our return date has been pushed back another five months. Everyone on the team is equally annoyed but there isn't much we can do. The stresses of the day-to-day seem to have made us all numb. At least at this point, we have a solid routine. A blessing and a curse, considering it's even easier to let our minds wander.

Charlie's birthday has once again rolled around and I haven't stopped thinking about her. The long days and endless nights have given me more than enough time to reflect on everything that has happened. It doesn't help that the loneliness is playing mind games that I wasn't prepared for. I'm starting to wonder if I've gotten to the point where I could forgive her for cheating. It still kills me to think that she would do that to me, but I also know that I didn't even give her a chance to explain.

I unblocked her about a week ago, craving any information I could get, but she hasn't posted in months. Not since I left her outside her apartment. Her social media shouldn't worry me as much as it does, but I can't stop myself from caring about her and from thinking about her all the time. I've typed out a hundred different emails but haven't sent any of them yet. Her birthday may be the day my resolve comes crashing down, though. *I fucking miss her.*

Walking out to the makeshift gym, I spot Drew out there, lifting weights with a zoned-out expression on his face.

When he looks up and gives me a nod, I decide to bite the bullet and ask him about her. I haven't mentioned her in a year. Not since her last birthday, when he caught me sulking out here.

"Hey, you call your sister today?"

He stares back, stone-faced, and then blinks it away. "I tried. She won't answer my calls."

"What do you mean she won't answer?" Every nerve ending in my body stands to attention; it's not like Charlie to ignore him or anyone. She'll say exactly what's on her mind, even if we don't like it.

He sets down his weights and huffs out a big breath of air. His jaw works back and forth as he grinds his teeth together. "You want to do this? Because you haven't wanted to talk about Charlie since we left."

Running my hand over the stubble on my jaw, I nod. "I know. I've been pissed and hurt. But that doesn't mean I stopped caring."

He sighs, backing down too. "Same. She hasn't responded to me. In her defense, I was pretty shitty toward her before we left. Then the first few months here were so chaotic, trying to find our footing, that I didn't really reach out. Around Thanksgiving, I realized I hadn't talked to her since we left, so I emailed, texted, and then called. When I still hadn't heard back by Christmas, I called mom. She lit my ass on fire, but she wouldn't say much. Only that, 'Charlie's fine.' I tried to push, but mom told me to drop it until Charlie was ready to talk to me."

"I didn't fucking ask you to do that!" Guilt mixed with frustration flows through me. I would never have asked him to not talk to Charlie; if anything, I tried to keep him out of it. They only have each other for immediate family. It must have nearly killed her to feel like she lost us both at the same time.

"Of course you didn't, asshole. But you're my best friend, and she's my sister. I'm allowed to be pissed when she fucks up. Cheating on you? Come on, that's no small offense."

My head hangs low as I try to shake away the confusing feelings. "I know. I *think* I know. Something about it feels off, though. My gut is telling me there's more to the story but my head saw it as clear as day."

"You saw a guy in her bed; it doesn't get more clear than that." He's right; it's probably the time messing with my head, distorting the memories. My brain wants there to be another reason to explain what happened. Although the alternative is that I left her there with an unwelcome man in her bed. Either way, I lose.

Feeling more confused than when I went in there, I went back to my room to call my mom. I've gotten enough lectures over the years to know when one is coming, and today will be no different. She tried to talk to me about Charlie when it first happened, but I wouldn't listen. Shut down every time she brought her up, then she stopped mentioning her at all.

She answers on the first ring and I do my best at small talk, even though it's killing me inside.

"Hey ma, I miss ya. How's home?"

"It's good. Hotter than Georgia asphalt, and not even June." She sounds like she's in a good mood at least.

"Yeah, it's pretty hot here too." Iraq isn't terrible in May, but when you add on the gear, it adds another layer of heat.

"You two staying safe?" Concern drips from her voice.

"We are. Not much going on right now. Wait and see. Feels like a lot of babysitting adults, making sure diplomats and their staff are safe." That's not exactly true, but I'm not allowed to go into details and I wouldn't want to worry my mom even if I could.

"I know how that goes."

"Anything else new with you? Talk to Ev or Odessa lately?" I'm fishing for information right now, hoping she may throw me a scrap.

"Yeah, Ev is back home already. Love's flying those birds, although he always has, so nothing new there. Dess is galli-vanting around the world, from job to job. This modeling thing is keeping her busy but she keeps me updated on where she's staying."

"That's good, and..."

"And? And, what?" Her no nonsense tone has me cringing. She's always been able to read my mind.

I relent, knowing it's about to bite me in the ass. "How 'bout Charlie?"

"She's fine." My eyebrows pinch together, knowing that is exactly what she told Drew. There's absolutely more going on than she's telling us.

"Alright. Just fine? Drew mentioned she hasn't responded to him in a while."

"Yep. Fine." She drawls out the word "fine" like it is anything but "fine."

"Mom..." She's not usually this tight-lipped about anything unless she's keeping a secret.

"Don't you 'mom' me! You two boys get my goose. Blowin' her off like that and then leavin'! Charlie is *fine*. I talked to her today and wished her a happy birthday."

Clenching my teeth together is the only thing keeping me from losing my cool at her vagueness. I know it won't help, though, my mother is nothing if not stubborn. If she's upset, there's no way she's going to let it go easily.

I take a deep breath through my nose and let it out. "Ok. I was worried. I didn't know Drew wasn't talking to her either. He told me today and said she wasn't responding."

An audible huff of air comes out of her nose. "We'll talk about it when you get home."

Shit. "Alright, I love ya."

"Love you too, Hayes. Stay safe over there, stay diligent."

Our call ends, and I'm left with even more anxiety than I had before.

I don't know if Charlie is pissed at me or if she even has a reason to be pissed at me. It sounds like she's pissed at Drew, too. Shutting him out like we did to her. The strangest part about everything, though, is that she's cut off social media for this long. She went from posting nearly every day to nothing since we left.

My resolve gives in and I send her an email, praying she will respond with at least proof of life.

"Happy Birthday, Charlie."

It takes all of me to not call her Sunshine. The old nickname wants to slip out like it always did. She was the sunniest part of my life, and then she was gone, taking the sunshine with her.

Chapter Nineteen

Charlie

Twenty-two feels good. Like a new chapter to put behind the old one. I've got Taylor Swift's 'Reputation' album jamming on my stereo, fueling my sass as I clean my house. Olivia is renting it to me for basically nothing, saying it's a perk to being her employee. Really, it's because she has a heart of gold and it was the first house available to get me out of the apartment I was in before.

The house is small but cute. Two bedrooms, with the master being much bigger than the other. It has a jack-and-jill bathroom between the two bedrooms. The living room and kitchen are connected into one big, outdated space. Thankfully, Olivia is giving me free range to do whatever I want with it.

I've taken my time going through each room, trying to get each one perfectly set up for my new life. The master bedroom has a spacious walk-in closet that has an attic door cut into the ceiling. I threw all my 'Hayes memories' up there and, metaphorically speaking, locked them away. It was really just a box of all the things he's given me or I've saved over the years. I don't have the heart to get rid of it, but I don't want to look at it every day either. So, into the creepy attic it goes. Where it can stay until he gets his shit together.

Dan and Levi helped bring my second-hand furniture over from my apartment the other day and it surprisingly fits well. I've been thrifting and stopping at every garage I've seen for months. A small thing to keep my mind busy, but searching for the perfect pieces has brought me so much joy. It's turned this little house into a little home, and I'm here for it.

Tonight, they've insisted on throwing me a "Turner-approved" birthday party at Olivia and Dan's. Well, Dan insisted. He's all about a party—really, any excuse to be social—and he's happy about it. Knowing him, he invited half the town and it's going to be a full house. The party that they threw when he became lieutenant last fall would have put a frat house to shame.

I'm nearly the last to arrive at the party, but only because everyone in this town is always early. They still live in the home that they bought when they first got married. It's a touch bigger than mine but completely updated. Olivia spent months working on it when they bought it, making every inch personal to them. If she wasn't so emotionally attached to it, I'm sure she'd already be in a bigger one by now. *Lord knows they could afford the biggest house in Central Oregon.*

I open the door and walk into a chorus of "Happy birthday!"

My grin widens as I do a shoulder shimmy and then shout, "Woohoo!" I've never been the girl who's embarrassed by stuff like this. Not that I need to be the center of attention all the time, but I do like when I get a little of it. Right now, there's a whole lot of people here to celebrate me and I'm relishing in it.

Olivia hugs me first, then Dan. Both of them are sporting cheshire grins that are starting to make me nervous.

"Welcome to a redo of your 21st birthday! Liv mentioned that your birthday last year was low-key. No one should have a 21st that they remember."

I glance around the room, now noticing all the party decorations say 21st birthday party. My eyes instantly go a little cloudy at the gesture. Last year, I was cut off from most of my best friends and barely made it to a birthday dinner with Connie. This year, an entire town showed up to celebrate my birthday.

Zeke, Dan's dad, hugs me next. He's the silver-fox version of Dan and Levi. He's got the charming yet authoritative vibe down to a t. "Happy birthday, Charlie! I'm taking the kids home with me after dessert so that you can party until sunrise."

"Not sure I'll make it that long, but I'll do my best!" I say, with a wink.

He chuckles back and then gets a serious look. "Whatever time it is, just make sure you don't drive. My contribution to the party is a hired driver. Anyone who drinks gets a ride home."

"Thanks, Zeke! That's so nice of you!" I give him another hug and he smiles bashfully before excusing himself to go play with the kids.

Outside on the patio, I spot Levi making drinks for Luke, Dan's partner and Luke's girlfriend, Madelyn. Luke and Madelyn couldn't be more opposite, from appearance to personality. Luke is all cowboy—gruff and rugged—while Madelyn is all city—perky and chic.

With an internal groan, I make my way out there to grab a drink and say hi. I've honestly never had a problem with Luke; it's Maddy who is the loose cannon. The more she drinks, the harder it is to be around her.

"CHARLIE! My third favorite girl! Happy birthday!" Levi shouts as soon as I step out of the sliding glass door. He's been calling me his third favorite girl since Ellie's birth. Ellie first, Olivia second, and me third.

I chuckle as I walk to stand by Luke and Madelyn. "Hey, y'all!"

Luke greets me with a head nod and gruffly says, "Happy birthday." Madelyn throws on her sweetest fake smile and high-pitched voice. "Happy birthday, Charlie! You look gorgeous!" If I didn't know any better, I'd swear I just saw both Levi *and* Luke cringe simultaneously.

"So do you! Thanks for coming!"

She smiles back and then asks, "What are you drinking? Levi is our bartender tonight and he makes the best cocktails!"

Levi rolls his eyes and shakes his head, ignoring her comment. He finishes shaking the mixer and pours the contents into two glasses before silently handing them to Luke and Madelyn. *Awkward.*

"Think I'll just have a beer for now. " I say as I turn to grab a beer from the cooler off to the side. "I should get back in there and say hey to everyone I missed."

Levi looks at me with pleading eyes, trying to silently tell me to stay but there's no way I'm getting into the middle of whatever I just walked out to. My guess is that Madelyn is a little too tipsy and a little too flirty. It's happened before and Levi always looks like he wishes a giant hole would appear to swallow him up. Meanwhile, Luke shuts down and tries to ignore it.

Back inside, I go back to greeting everyone and thanking them for coming. It takes nearly thirty minutes but finally I get to the last person, Maisie.

She owns our favorite coffee hut in town. Olivia and I will

drive across Three Sisters, bypassing every other drive-thru, to get her coffee. She's delicately setting out desserts from a box that she must have brought.

"Please tell me you made all those." I ask with drool practically dripping out of my mouth.

She grins, her bubbly personality coming out. "I did! All your favorites—cream cheese brownies, danishes, and red velvet cupcakes."

"Eek! I love you so much! Thanks, Mais!"

"Hey, birthday girl! Come do a shot with us!" The bad influence twin shouts through the open sliding glass door.

Letting out a groan, I look at the chaos that is happening out back. Levi is handing out shot glasses and then pouring a very expensive bottle of tequila into each one. He knows it's my favorite and the only way I'll actually concede to this.

"Fine! But if I barf tonight, you're holding my hair!"

He gives me a playful smile. "Wouldn't be the first time I rescued a drunk princess."

"Yeah, yeah. You got any banana bags for my hangover tomorrow?" Another good thing about being friends with this group is that there isn't a shortage of expensive liquor or trained professionals with access to medical supplies.

"He's coming to my house first!" Sweet, innocent Elise isn't as innocent as I thought she would be when I first met her. Despite the fact that she's old enough to be my grandmother, she drinks like a fish.

She holds up her shot glass, full of Fortaleza. "A toast to our favorite southern belle! When I fell that day, I'm beyond grateful that you were there to pick me up. Even more grateful that you decided to stay in town, and become one of us. Happy birthday, Charlie!" She downs her shot and we all follow. As soon as the heat reaches my throat, I know I'm in for a long night.

I've had more than my fair share of liquor when I hear a knock on the door.

I open it, only to find a giant, gorgeous man staring down at me. His dirty blonde hair is shorter on the sides and longer on top, but styled to perfection. The stubble beard, mixed with the blue/green eyes, has got to be every woman's fantasy. He is 6ft 5in of all man. I feel like I'm finally starting to understand the saying, "Climb him like a tree."

The tequila must be hitting harder than I thought, because I shout out, "Did someone order me a stripper for my birthday?" *Because yes, please.*

He looks at me bewilderedly, like he was definitely not expecting me to answer the door or make an idiot of myself.

"Hey, uh, sorry I was looking for Olivia." He glances into the house, now noticing a full party going on, and his eyes grow wide. He moves his shoulder back protectively and I notice the infant carrier he's holding.

"Ethan!" Olivia rushes around the kitchen counter to greet our new guest. That's when she sees the car seat and nearly trips over her feet. "Woah, since when did you multiply?"

He grins and looks around the full room. "Guess it wasn't going to be long before the town found out anyway. Everyone, this is Jake. My son."

The entire group jumps to their feet, rushing to the front, trying to greet Ethan and Jake.

Everyone, but Maisie.

I move around the crowd and toward her. Her eyes begin darting around the room and her lower lip starts slightly shaking.

"What's wrong?"

She startles and her eyes snap to me, like she's just now

noticing I'm here even though I'm only a foot away. "He's back."

Based on her facial expression, it isn't a good thing either. A single tear falls down her cheek and she quickly brushes it away.

"I really need to go." She looks around panicked, trying to find an exit but Ethan's massive form and fifteen other people are blocking her only chance of escape.

Grabbing her hand, I pull her toward the door that leads into the garage. Once the light is flipped on, we step down and stand next to Olivia's old Jeep.

Before she could get around me, I wrapped my arms around her shoulders and hugged her. "Are you okay? Is he an ex or something?"

"I'll be okay. No, we never..." She shakes her head, trailing off into a different thought. "I'm just shocked. I haven't seen him or heard from him in *years*. I didn't even know he was with someone and now they have a baby."

I know it was more than she's leading on but whatever Maisie and he had or didn't have isn't my business. I can tell just his being here is wrecking her. Long gone is the bubbly, charismatic Maisie; in her place is a heartbroken woman.

My heart goes out to her, knowing I'd feel the same way if Hayes ever walked in carrying a tiny baby.

"I don't know what went down with you two, but call me anytime. Day or night. I'm here if you need to vent; a shoulder to cry on; or someone to down shots and dance on a table with."

She nods and tears well in her eyes as she takes the opportunity to leave through the side door.

When I got back into the house, things seemed to have calmed down. Everyone was still asking a million questions, but Ethan seemed to be evading most of them. He'd only say that he has full custody and Jake's mom isn't in the picture. I also caught him watching the garage door that Maisie used more than once. Each time, disappointment briefly clouded his eyes before he quickly blinked it away.

Chapter Twenty

Charlie

Thursday, November 29.

My monthly phone call to Connie is today, and I'm dreading it. For no other reason than it's about time to face the music. The guys are coming up on 18 months gone, so they should be home any day. Which means she will be telling them the entire story. I'm not sure if I'm ready for them to know where I am, though. I'm living in this happy bubble, and the second they know, I'll have to face the reality of everything.

I miss them—all of them, really. Drew, Hayes, Everett, and Odessa. But I still talk to Odessa occasionally. She's still traveling all over, rubbing elbows with the rich and famous. The last time I talked to her, she was on a yacht somewhere in the Med, living her best life.

It's been a full year since I went back for the trial. I thought that it would be no problem going back but I hadn't realized the setback it would put on my new life. It was weeks before I felt safe again. Eventually, the nightmares became fewer and further between and I wasn't watching over my shoulder as often. The ache in my heart began to dull as well, and survival mode turned off. It was around then that I stopped thinking of Heartsville as home. Now, home is Three Sisters, where my heart and soul feel at ease.

The only thing that's missing is Hayes. My heart still only beats for him, which infuriates me. I wanted to have moved on by now; let him go. He treated me like I was less than—less than a girlfriend, less than a best friend, less than a human, let alone his soulmate. I'm not less than, and I refuse to let anyone treat me like that, even Hayes.

At this point, I don't know if he even cares to hear the truth or if he's still in such a blind rage that he won't even listen to the facts. Hayes has never been one to lose his cool over anything. The man wrote the book on how to handle stressful situations, but that night I saw a different version of him. I don't know if being in the Navy has changed him, or maybe it's all the things he's seen, but I don't want to be with someone who doesn't trust me.

So yes, maybe I'm being a little petty and hiding out. Maybe I want him to suffer a little bit so that he understands how it feels to be shut down without a chance to clarify. The same goes for Drew. Both of them condemned me before even hearing my side of things. They deserve to sweat a little bit and think about how shitty they've both treated me. There's no way I'm about to make it easier on the two men who should have given me the benefit of the doubt. *I hope their ignorant egos get a big dose of humble pie.*

After an hour of contemplating how to say that eloquently to Connie, I finally take a deep breath and call her.

She answers on the first ring. "Hey, sweet girl. How ya doin'?"

Just hearing her voice brings tears to my eyes. I act all tough but the second I talk to her, I'm a big pile of mush that misses her.

"I'm doing good. Things have been busy. Did you have a good Thanksgiving?"

"It was good. The Parkinson's invited me over for dinner so that was nice. They have just had their fifth grand-baby, a little boy." I grin, knowing the insinuation she's trying to make. Connie has wanted grand-babies for years. She's never outright said it, but with each passing year, the hints become more obvious. Before Hayes ended things, I would have thought we would be married by now and talking about having our own babies soon. *What a joke that is.*

"Good for them. I bet it's nice being surrounded by all that love."

"How's baby Ellie? Did she have a good birthday party?" Connie doesn't know exactly where I am, but she does know everything going on in my life. I've given her enough information that, with a couple Google searches, she'd easily be able to figure it out. I've always trusted her to keep it quiet though. She has a similar "stick-it-to-'em" attitude that I have. No doubt she wants the guys to suffer a little bit as well.

Ellie just turned one and is developing the biggest personality already. Temper tantrums for days, the center of attention, and the cutest thing in the world. Laughing, I say, "She's the best. Sassy and sweet already. Dan invited the whole town and Ellie really hammed it up with him."

"And how's Ben?"

"He's doin' good. He loves going to school. His Pre-K teacher thinks he's already too advanced for the class."

"Hayes was like that. Only time he sat still was if he had a book in front of him." I ignored the tiny pang in my heart at the mention of his name.

"I don't doubt that. Speaking of Hayes, shouldn't they be

home soon?" I try to sound as unaffected as possible, but even I can hear the slight tremor in my voice when I say his name.

"Tomorrow actually. You ready to talk to them? I think they need to hear your story from you."

I shake my head, tears rolling down my cheeks without me even realizing it. "No. If they ask, then you can tell them what happened with Carter and why I left. I don't want them to worry. I'm safe and happy. But I'm not ready. They'll need time to process the trauma I went through. I'm just... I'm not in a place where I can handle all their emotions and my own. Once they've both had a chance to wrap their heads around it, I'll add them to the app." Where I can keep some distance. I know that I'm a pushover when it comes to Hayes. I'll lose my grudge the second I hear that deep voice.

"You're wise beyond your years, Charlie. Setting up a strong boundary is important, but I know those boys, and they have always been boundary pushers. I'll do my best to make sure they give you a little time. My lips are sealed with everything you've told me. But if I know Hayes, come hell or high water, that boy is going to find you."

I wish I was strong enough to say that thought didn't excite me. Part of me wants to hate him and the other part is still craving his love. What he does with the information when Connie tells him is on him, though. He may even have a girl-friend at this point—not sure how much dating there was wher-ever he went, but stranger things have happened, i.e., my insane stalker. Either way, I'm not putting too much hope into Hayes. I've already been disappointed once by his choices; if he rejects me again, I don't know if I can recover.

"I love you. Thank you for supporting me throughout all of this. You've let me do things my way, even if you didn't always agree. I will always be grateful for how much you've helped me."

"Oh, hush, dear. You'll make me cry. I've loved you since the day your momma told me she was giving us all a girl. We didn't know how much we needed it at the time— being surrounded by those rough and tumble boys—but you were everything we could have wanted and more." *Cue the waterfalls of tears.*

<hr>

Barely sleeping last night, I dragged myself into the office. Olivia is already sitting at her desk, and Ellie is coloring at her little table.

Ellie sees me first and says, "AuCha!" Her version of Aunt Char. She lifts up her Elsa coloring page and grins at me. It's one giant scribbled mess of colors, but I can't help not to smile at how proud she is.

"I love it!" I say before I kiss her on the top of her head and head to my desk.

I drop my purse onto the surface and it opens, causing all of the contents to spill out. Most of it is junk— a protein bar, some loose coins, and a pen— but my eyes get stuck on the thing I try to forget is in there. The antique mint tin. I haven't pulled it out of my purse since I found it in there when I left South Carolina. Occasionally, I'll open my purse and get a small whiff of peppermint—the smell alone almost makes me cry—but usually I simply pretend it isn't there.

"You look like shit." Olivia says with a grin, teasing me.

I roll my eyes, but still laugh. I have no doubt I look rough right now. No makeup, hair thrown in a messy bun, and my shirt already has a coffee stain.

"Couldn't sleep."

"Anything to do with a certain someone that you mentioned may be home soon? I'm waiting for the day he shows up and swoops you out of this office." *A thought I've fantasized about a million times.*

"I talked to Connie yesterday. They'll be in Heartsville sometime today."

Olivia's smile falters. "Are you going to call them? Or is she going to tell them?"

"I told her she could tell them if they asked, but that we should all take some time to digest the situation."

"Do you think they'll do that? They don't exactly seem like 'wait and see' kind of guys."

I shake my head and then shrug my shoulders as I throw the contents that spilled out of my purse back into it. "You know what? Not my problem. I'm safe here. If they want to waste their time trying to find me instead of being patient for *one* month, then that's on them."

Her mischievous grin lights up her face. "Well, I hope he decides to pull his head out of his ass and come riding in on that white horse with the biggest apology known to mankind."

"Ugh. Me too. Even though I'm pissed and want to make him suffer."

Olivia knows everything—all my struggles. How much I still love Hayes. How annoyed I am at Drew for ignoring me. How scared I am that things won't go back to normal. She's a best friend through and through. There to talk shit about them when I need it, push back when I'm too irrational in my feelings, but no matter what, she always has my best interests at heart.

"Nothing wrong with making him sweat it out a bit. But I know how much you love him and how much time has already been lost. Whatever you decide, I've got your back."

"He may not even ask about me and all of this stress will be for nothing."

She scoffs in my direction but continues to type on her computer. "I bet the first thing he asks about is you."

One can only hope.

"Does this bring up any of the Carter stuff? I know you've tried to bury the situation down deep but I can only imagine how Hayes being back will resurface it all."

My stomach churns at the thought. "Yeah. Everything is officially coming to a head. Carter's probably lucky he's in prison. Two trained snipers with a vendetta and he'd be dead within twenty four hours of them getting back."

One of her shoulders raises slightly as she nonchalantly says, "Probably wouldn't be a bad thing in that creeps case."

Agreed, Liv. Agreed.

Chapter Twenty-One

Hayes

The smell of fresh cinnamon rolls mixed with bacon hits my nose as I open the door to my mom's house.

"Ma!" I bellow as she comes out of the hallway.

Drew shoves me from behind, trying to get to Mom first. I hook my left leg around his right before he can, though, effectively tripping him.

I throw my arms around my mom, pulling her into me while she laughs. "Missed ya, mom!"

Drew takes her from me and plants a kiss on her cheek. "But I missed you more." We've always been like this, pretending to fight to be my mom's favorite.

"Come on, boys! You two are as thin as a fiddle string." She brings us into the kitchen and shows off the entire feast she's made. Sausage links, patties, and bacon fill up an entire tray. Scrambled and fried eggs rest on another. Waffles, hash browns, cinnamon rolls, and muffins are placed throughout.

"You invite the neighborhood?" Drew asks mom incredulously.

"Nope, just know how much you two can eat, and I haven't

been able to cook for anyone for a while. I was too excited this morning to sleep, so I made all your favorites!"

He laughs and shakes his head. "I will devour it all, single-handedly if I have to. Where's Char at though?"

Just hearing her name sends chills through my body. Neither of us have heard back from her and I've sent more than one message on her birthday. The fact she hasn't responded yet only made us try harder. We even tried to go around my mom, but Everett said he hadn't talked to her since her twenty-first birthday and Odessa was taking a similar route as my mom, avoiding the topic all together.

"Let's start eating and then we will talk." She makes a beeline for the kitchen without looking our way.

My hackles instantly raise and Drew must have the same feeling because he looks at me with a familiar sense of unease.

We grab a plate, fill it up high, and then say grace.

As soon as mom is done with the prayer, I start my inquisition.

"Where's Charlie?"

Mom squares her shoulders and lifts her chin, meeting my gaze with determination.

"Charlie decided that she needed a break and a fresh start somewhere new. She borrowed the motorhome at first, but when she found a place she wanted to stay, she brought it back." The fork I was holding slips from my hand and lands on the glass plate with a loud clatter.

Drew's says, "What the fuck?" At the same time, I'm saying, "Why the fuck didn't you tell us?"

"I'll excuse your language toward me this time, but don't you boys let it happen again." She scolds us like we are fifteen instead of twenty-seven.

"Charlotte asked me not to tell you until you were home safely. *She* was worried about you *two*. She calls once a month through an app, like clockwork. I spoke to her yesterday."

Drew's thumbs begin their rhythmic tapping on the table as he asks, "Why an app?"

"She doesn't want anyone to know where she is. It's one of those untraceable data scrambling ones. She gave me permission to tell you what happened, but I need you both to promise you will not fly off the handle. You will sit, eat, and listen."

My eyes instantly snapped to Drew's; neither of us prepared for what's coming.

"Charlie was attacked by her neighbor, Carter Burch. He developed an obsession with her and then broke into her home. Twice." She gives me a pointed look, while my stomach rolls with nausea.

"You were there for the first break-in. The second time, she was in the shower. He was standing in her bathroom when she got out. She, well, to be frank, beat the shit out of him."

All the emotions hit me like a ton of bricks as my brain churns over the details my mom continues to share. I got it so wrong. I left my girlfriend, the love of my life, in danger because I was poisoned to believe that she would cheat on me. That's what everyone around you tells you. There are no faithful women. They all cheat while you're deployed, training, or doing whatever the hell the Navy tells you to be doing.

I've hated her. I've missed her like crazy. I've spent the last eighteen months going over every detail of that night. The look of betrayal she gave me. The sadness when I didn't believe her. The memory mixes with the sight of that guy in her bed, the flowers everywhere, and her scared look. I thought it was just because she'd been caught. But, no. It was because some man had broken into her apartment and violated her space. And then, to top it all off, I left her there with him.

Drews thumbs up the pace, but he hasn't said anything.

Neither of us has eaten a single bite as we stare at the food. The guilt and shame we both suddenly possess hover between us in the air, heavy and suffocating.

"The police found him knocked out in her bathroom. He was taken to the hospital and then booked. She left a few days after that and hasn't wanted anyone to know where she is. She came home for the trial and testified but flew back out the day after."

"He in jail now?" Drew looks up, and I know exactly what he's thinking and why he's asking. *If he's out, he's dead.*

Mom nods her head and says, "Prison. Because of his previous offense, they gave him five years, but he could be out sooner."

"Previous offense?" I growl out.

"A similar thing happened before. He was obsessed with a girl but they were minors. He got away with a slap on the wrist. Although, Harvard did revoke his admission and scholarship. He's as smart as he is evil, a dangerous combination."

"For fuck's sake!" Drew slams his palms on the table and stands up.

My mom arches one eyebrow but doesn't say anything. He sits back down and takes a deep breath, puffing his cheeks out and shaking his head while he huffs.

When he looks calm again, I say to my mom, "I need to talk to her."

"No."

My jaw clenched so hard that it tickled, but I waited for her to continue.

"I told her yesterday that you'd be in town and she said she would think about talking to you next month. I know it sounds hard, but I'm respecting her wishes."

I nod my head despite knowing full and well that I will not be respecting her wishes. I'm finding her today. Hopping on a flight and bringing her back home. If it means not renewing my Navy contract and getting out, then so be it.

I will fix this mistake.

Drew and I both start texting under the table, formulating a plan. Now that we know she's hiding, we can put all of our energy into finding her over the next few days. Considering the two of us have more skills and connections than most, we should be able to find her before Drew has to be back in California.

Three days later, Drew and I were in the same spot as the day we found out. We each spent hours breaking into her accounts, only to find each one had been inactive since her twenty-first birthday. I was able to get the name of the app that she's been using to talk to my mom and Odessa, but beyond that, I have no idea how to add her or unscramble the data. Charlie completely vanished and turned into a ghost in the wind.

Drew and I finally decided it was time to call in reinforcements and head back to California. He has a big Team move coming up, and I need to put in my exit packet. Before we left, though, we both agreed we needed to meet with one person before we left.

Detective Paul. A portly man who looks like he's close to retiring. The first time I called him, he laughed for nearly three minutes. His exact words were, "Your momma told me this would happen. You'd call and try to raise all sorts of hell to find your girl. Well, I got news for ya son; I don't know where she's at." His southern accent was so thick that even I had a hard time understanding him. He did agree to meet with us, though, so on our way to the airport, we stopped by the Columbia Police Department to have a chat.

When we got there, he grinned from ear to ear at first. It wasn't until we sat down in his office and he opened up the file that his smile disappeared. His entire demeanor flipped the second he looked at the first page.

"Here's the deal. Carter Burch is a spoilt-rich, arrogant, son-of-a-bitch. He's also smart, as all get out."

Drew and I tensed simultaneously, our muscles locking tight as we listened to him. We're both sitting in chairs, facing a man who is supposed to tell us we shouldn't be worried; however, he's doing the complete opposite.

"He was raised by his paternal grandparents from birth and they gave him whatever he wanted. When Charlie didn't immediately fawn all over him, it fueled his obsession. We searched his apartment. It was worse than you could imagine— worse than we wanted Charlie to even know. After she gave her testimony, we asked her to step out of the courtroom. I don't know if she would have ever recovered after seeing all the images he had of her. He broke into the front office of the complex, made a duplicate key to her apartment, and then hid at least fifteen cameras all over her apartment."

"Fucking hell." Drew groans from the seat next to me.

I can't even respond right now; my jaw is clenched so hard that I'm going to need dental work. The haze of anger clouds my better judgment and all I can think about is how the hell I'm going to kill this guy. I don't even care if I get away with it. No man who does that deserves to walk this earth, even if he is walking it behind bars.

"Leaving town was the best thing she could have done for her mental health. When I first met her, she was scared and broken. The woman who came back to testify was a woman with strength and resilience. She walked into the courtroom with her head held so high that I knew she could overcome anything life threw at her." He let out a mirthless laugh and the corner of his mouth lifted slightly. "Well, that, and I saw the aftermath of what she did to him. He looked like he had gone ten rounds with a trained cage fighter when I interviewed him."

I feel my body slightly begin to relax. My breathing and heart rate started to return to normal. I'm so damn glad she kicked his ass, even though I wish she had never had to.

"What do we do now? He has a few more years left?" I ask, trying to gauge what Detective Paul thinks will happen in the future.

A long sigh comes from him and then he shakes his head. "With good behavior, it could be less. I don't have an answer to what you should do. If she were my wife..." He looks up at his closed door and then looks me dead in the eye. "Well, I wouldn't hold this position any longer if she were my wife. He belongs back with the devil, where he came from."

Drew and I exchange knowing glances. This guy is lucky he's in prison.

Chapter Twenty-Two

Hayes

Monday, December 3.

Things have moved quickly since I got back to San Diego. I don't know what I was expecting, but not for everything to happen as fast as it did. It's official. I'm leaving the Navy. I'm finding my girl. Then I'm getting her ass back to South Carolina, where she belongs—where we both belong, together.

It took me two days to get all the information filled out and filed with my chain of command. They plan on expediting my paperwork so I can be out of here in under a month. It gives me a little bit of time to find Charlie, pack up my condo, and say "see ya later" to my best friend. Never goodbye. Again, something our dad's started. Even on my dad's death bed, Uncle Jesse just kept repeating that he'd "see ya later."

Drew and I had the privilege to spend seven years on a team together. It was a miracle that we even stayed together this long and got to serve side by side, like our dads did. Always wondered if they had something to do with that, pulling strings from up above.

Now, Drew is moving to another team that needs help. They've lost some guys and are in desperate need of some experience to help rebuild. I feel for him that he's already heading back out again so soon, but he's built differently than I am. He keeps his emotions buried so deeply that even I have a hard time telling where his head is sometimes.

"You nervous about switching?" I ask while packing up the few things I have.

He scoffs and shakes his head. "Nah, same shit, different teammates. It'll be alright. I'm only worried about Charlie at this point."

"You and I, both. I can't believe she's been hiding for almost two fucking years." She's always been stubborn as hell and even more independent, but this is a new extreme.

"Always was the goddamn hide and seek champ. Remember when she hid in the laundry basket in the closet for like four hours?"

I chuckle at the memory. Our parents were so mad when we came to them and said we couldn't find her. Even they looked for an hour, almost calling the police at one point. I was the one who found her curled up in the bottom of my laundry basket, snoring softly. The physical relief I felt when I saw that strawberry blonde hair hiding beneath my dirty clothes is something I'll never forget. We were always watchful of her, but after that moment, a protective switch flipped. I was probably no older than ten, but even so, that little scare gave me a sense of responsibility and protectiveness that has stuck with me ever since. It was the first innocent seed planted right into my heart, eventually growing into a deep-rooted love. A love that I let down by not doing the one thing that I promised myself I'd always do. Protect her.

The guilt and anger have been crushing me. If I wasn't so focused on trying to find her, I'd be in a self-deprecating spiral of regret and shame. The anger I feel toward myself only rivals the anger I feel toward the man who put us in this situation. If I dwell on that, though, I'll end up finding a way to murder the bastard. My first priority has to be Charlie, and only Charlie. Dealing with him can wait until he's out of prison and it's easier to make him disappear.

Drew must have gotten lost in his own thoughts as well, because neither of us have said anything for a while. Both of us are folding and packing things away like we've done a hundred times before.

He breaks the silence first: "This isn't your fault, you know?" *Except, it is.*

My fingers freeze on the shirt I was folding. We haven't talked much about the events that led to Charlie running away or how either of us handled it before we knew. How he could think this isn't my fault is beyond me. I should have never left her. I should have trusted her. I should have killed him the second I saw how scared she was.

When I finally look at him, I see the indistinguishable pain and guilt I've been feeling for days reflecting on his face. The tiredness weighing on him makes him look years older than we are. I've been too focused on myself and Charlie to see how it's affecting her brother.

"Not your fault, either." I try to throw as much sincerity into my voice as I can. Drew has always had a tough exterior, hiding his emotions behind the ego he pretends to have. I've known him my entire life, though, and I know he only put on the mask to hide how devastated he was when he lost his parents.

"I fucked up. I'm all she has left, and I ignored her. If I'd been there, maybe she wouldn't have left."

I nod my head; he's not wrong, and I'm not about to lie to him to make him feel better. "Maybe, maybe not. Charlie's always been headstrong. If she wasn't comfortable staying, she wouldn't have. I'm the one who left her with that psycho in her room. I'll never forgive myself for that, but I can't focus on that until we know she's safe."

He looks away, taking a deep breath through his nose. You'd think we'd both be numb after all the shit we've done and seen over the last few years, but this hits differently. It's personal.

When he looks back, the corner of his lip turns up. "Alibi, and hide the body."

"Always, man." A humorless laugh shakes my chest. I haven't heard that in years, but we used to say it to Everett all the time. His dad was an abusive asshole and we made a pact that if he ever went after Odessa, he was dead. Thankfully, it never came to that and Odessa pretty much moved in with my mom after we graduated high school. I don't think Ev would have even joined the Army if she hadn't.

Three weeks later, not much has changed. Drew left for a training exercise this morning and we officially said our "see ya laters."

I wake up every day, hoping that today is the day that I find her. I've called everyone I know who knows Charlie and no one seems to know where she is or has talked to her in nearly two years. Well, everyone but my mom and Odessa. However, those two won't say a damn thing about where she is. They just keep telling me to be patient and wait until she calls. I don't want to wait another week to find out whether or not she's agreed to add me to her app, though. I need to see her. Face-to-face. I need to see that she's okay and beg her to forgive me.

She's hidden so well that even our reinforcement, Lincoln, is having a hard time finding her—and Lincoln can find anyone. He was a great SEAL but he's even more badass when it comes to computers and hacking into secure data. The whole team felt his loss when he was medevaced out, but the only thing we cared about was that he was alive. They were able to save his leg, but it did end his career early.

I was finally able to get a hold of him last week and explain to him what was going on. He told me he needed a few days to work on it, but he was confident that he'd be able to track her down. Meanwhile, I sat around in my empty condo, waiting for news.

It's the day after Christmas when I finally get the call I've been waiting for.

"Carrington, I found her."

I throw my legs off the couch, sitting up. "You're fucking kidding."

A low chuckle comes through the phone. "Nope. You know anyone in Three Sisters, Oregon?"

"I've never even heard of that place." *Why the hell would she be in Oregon of all places?*

"I hadn't either, but that's where she is. Her flight from South Carolina was to Portland. I hacked the airport security footage. A white SUV picked her up with an Oregon license plate—541BEO. Oregon Database has that registered to Olivia Turner. I'll send you all the info I have on her."

"Holy shit." He fucking did it. He found Charlie, and she's not that far from me.

"Yep. When you see her, give her my props. She went almost 100% off the grid for almost two years. If she hadn't taken that flight, I don't know if I would've ever found her." It's a little reassuring that he even struggled to find her. I was starting to doubt my abilities.

"Thanks, man. I owe you one."

He scoffs in the background. "You saved my life. This was the least I could do."

"Would do it again in a second. Glad you're doing good, Linc. When all this is settled, we're getting a beer together."

Ending the call, I jump out of bed, shower, and then start packing my truck.

After I've been on the road for several hours, I call the business number Linc gave me.

A younger-sounding woman answers on the third ring, "Hello?"

"Mrs. Turner? This is Hayes Carrington. May I speak to Charlotte?"

The woman emits a tiny gasp, barely audible over the phone, before correcting herself. "Sorry, no one works here with that name."

"You sure about that?" I know she's lying, but I decide to play along.

"Yep." Her curt tone has me wanting to dig for more, but I choose to let it go. Unbeknownst to her, I already have all the information I need to know and I'm already well on my way to Oregon.

Chapter Twenty-Three

Hayes

Sixteen hours later, a large green sign welcomes me into the tiny town in the middle of Oregon. Three Sisters, Oregon, Cascadia County, Population: 2500.

Rolling into this tiny town in the middle of Oregon has adrenaline coursing through my veins. Traffic is backed up as the highway runs through the main part of town, giving me time to scope everything out. If it weren't for the tourists strolling along the main strip, I'd stick out like a sore thumb.

I can feel it in my gut that Charlie is still here. The woman I called denied that she knew Charlie, but there was something off in her tone. That, and Lincoln swears she's still here.

Now that I'm officially a civilian, I'll drive through every city if I have to in order to find her. She shouldn't be on the run. She should be home and looked out for. Even if she never forgives me and we don't get back together, I'll make sure she's safe. I owe her that. But I really fucking hope she forgives me.

I pull into a small hotel that looks more like a ski lodge than a hotel. The hotel attendant is just another teenage girl, bubbly and welcoming. I don't pay her much attention; I just hand over my card and wait for my room key. My eyes scan out the front window, watching for any sign of Charlie. I'd be lying if I said I wasn't disappointed that she wasn't one of the many that walked by.

Throwing my bag on the bed, I grab a quick shower and then get dressed. I've researched every part of this town. I know where every road is, where I *think* she's working, and possible places she would hang out.

My phone lights up and the vibration sounds on the wood nightstand.

"Hey, mom." I answered with less than enthusiasm. I drove through the entire seventeen hours to get here, only stopping for food and gas. I'm exhausted and energized all at the same time.

"How's it going, honey? You about to hit the road again?"

I clear my throat, ready for the verbal smackdown. "No. I just checked into the hotel."

"Hayes Carrington! You killing yourself to get to a town you don't even know if she's in won't solve a damn thing."

I'm a trained Navy SEAL. I've gone days without sleeping or eating—pushing myself until I physically felt like I couldn't move anymore, and then pushing myself harder. One long drive is nothing.

However, arguing with my concerned mother won't help.

"Sorry, mom. The adrenaline hit and I wouldn't have been able to sleep knowing I'm so close."

I hear a loud sigh on the other end. "Fine. You be careful, okay? She's happy, wherever she is. It's not your place to go in there demanding anything."

I've already run through every scenario in my mind, so it doesn't sting to hear her say that. She's been living here for a long time and has started a completely new life. I know that might not be a life that I fit into. It won't stop me from trying like hell, though.

I walked through the entire town fifteen times. Coming back to the same two-story brick building with the Cascades Property Management sign out front. It's Saturday, so it's been empty the entire time. My instincts are screaming at me that this is where she is, where she's working, and where she's been hiding. All that I want to do is buy a lawn chair and plant myself in the parking lot until Monday morning. It's almost dark and the beginning of winter, though, so I make my way to the small diner I passed a few times. I need to warm up a bit, eat some food, and get a better plan.

When I walk past the window, I look inside, scanning the room. *Old habits die hard.*

My eyes glaze over the booths—a family sitting with a baby, a woman with short hair sitting by herself in the booth, and two older gentlemen sitting behind her.

The air ceases to pump through my lungs as I do a double take on the strawberry blonde sitting alone.

There she is. By herself, eating a cheeseburger. I stare at her for at least a minute, trying to decide if my exhaustion has caused me to hallucinate her or if she's really there. Her hair is much shorter than when I left, barely touching her shoulders, but it's definitely her.

Taking a deep breath, I step inside in a daze. The door chimes and it snaps me back into reality. I glance around the front; there isn't anyone at the hostess station, so I turn toward Charlie again.

She takes a bite of her cheeseburger, staring at the table like she's completely lost in thought.

Six large steps and then I slide into the booth.

Her startled eyes look up at me, and then she chokes on her

bite of food. Coughing and spluttering, she reaches for her water.

"Fuck, Sunshine! Are you okay?" I try to stand up, but the table between us prevents me from doing much. My arm automatically stretches out, but I don't touch her. My hand dangles right next to her bicep, ready to haul her over the table if she needs the Heimlich.

I'm so focused on making sure she can breathe that I don't notice the person now standing by our table. Within a second, my outstretched arm is being nearly ripped out of its socket as I'm hauled out of the booth and thrown on the ground.

My cheek hits the cool, dirty tile as my arm is pinned behind my back. Cold metal snaps around my wrist, and in an instant I make the decision to lay still. I'm in a restaurant full of civilians, and startled gasps are starting to ricochet around the room. I know that I could easily get out of this lackluster hold, but resisting whatever this is will only cause more chaos.

Charlie starts coughing again and yelling, "Dan! No!"

"You know this guy?" I look over my shoulder to see the man talking. Lieutenant Turner, Cascadia Sheriff Department. From my research, he's the one married to her, now confirmed, boss.

A small smile tugs at my lips as I lay on the floor. I should be pissed as hell at this guy, but instead, I'm only happy that she has people looking out for her. I'd only been in that booth for ten seconds before he had me on the ground.

"It's Hayes! That's Hayes!" I turn my head again so I can see Charlie. Her face is bright red, her knees are on the booth, and she looks like she's frantically trying to get control of the situation.

Dan lets out a light chuckle and then helps me up. He removes the cuff and pats me on the shoulder. "Sorry 'bout that.

I was driving by when I saw you watching from outside. Thought you might be the villain in her story."

Oh, buddy, if you only knew. I might not be the villain who put her in this situation, but that doesn't make me the hero either.

Turning to face him, I give him a quick once-over. I don't know if I was distracted by finally getting to Charlie or if the adrenaline hit him hard, but I'm surprised that he was able to take me down so easily. He's a little shorter than me, and I've got at least fifty pounds of muscle on him.

I grin and extend my hand for him to shake. "Just glad someone's looking out for her."

He shakes my hand but then looks at Charlie. "You okay? Want me to stay close?"

She shakes her head, and tears fill her eyes. "No, I'm safe with Hayes."

Pride fills my chest as I hear her words. It's a relief to know that she still trusts me to keep her safe, despite all the mistakes I made. I was expecting her to be angry, yell, and storm out of here. Not to look at me the same way she did before all this happened.

I gesture with my head back toward the table, and we sit. I stay quiet, trying to ignore the million questions I have running through my mind. I'm sure she has just as many, and I want to give her the opportunity to ask them first.

Chapter Twenty-Four

Charlie

"What are you doing here?!"

I stare at the man I love with my entire heart and soul. Hayes not only appeared out of thin air, but he marched in and sat down at my booth without any hesitation.

As if he hadn't been out of my life for almost two years.

As if he hadn't left me scared and broken, standing on the sidewalk, begging for him to believe me.

As if he hadn't gone into some war-torn country, and I wasn't here wondering every single day if he was dead or alive —if he still hated me.

His eyes bore into mine with a mix of intensity and vulnerability, causing my heart to race and my breath to catch in my throat.

I hate how different he looks—drained and sad. I hate that I don't know if something happened on his deployment or if it was me leaving. Either way, he looks like a shell of himself. He's leaned out, and the dark shadows under his eyes look haunted. New creases line his eyes, and his smile doesn't lift as high as it once did. He looks like he's aged ten years in less than two.

I want to pull him into my arms and reassure him that everything is going to be okay, but I stop myself. There's a reason we haven't talked in nearly two years, and that's because Hayes walked out.

Sandra, my favorite server, stops by the table before he can answer. She looks like she's worked here for fifty years, and probably has. Her gray hair is always pulled into a bun, and her glasses ride low on the bridge of her nose.

"All good here?" She raises her silver eyebrow at me, and I almost laugh. *This town has my back through and through.*

I nod and give her a warm smile. "This is Hayes." I contemplate adding more, but saying he's my ex-boyfriend might kill me.

Looking back at Hayes, he hasn't taken his eyes off me. "He'll have the same thing as me. No tomatoes, please." He needs the calories, whether he's hungry or not. I haven't seen him this defined in years. He looks like he doesn't have an ounce of fat on him—all muscle and sharp angles.

A corner of his lip lifts in a half-smile as he nods in agreement. Sandra jots down his order and heads back to the kitchen, leaving Hayes and me alone at the table.

I can feel the weight of unspoken words hanging in the air. I lift an eyebrow, waiting for him to answer my question.

"I'm here to apologize." *Knife meets heart.* I don't know what I expected him to say, but leading with that feels cold and distant.

"Okay." I try to avoid the disappointment I'm feeling by looking out at the restaurant. "How'd you even find me?"

"I had some help. Do you remember Lincoln?" I nod my head in response. "He was sent home early from Iraq. RPG attack. Some shrapnel struck him in the thigh. It ended his career."

"Oh no! But he's okay?"

The corner of his mouth pulls up a bit, and he's bobbing his head with nervousness. "Yeah, full recovery. So, he's, uh, well, he's remarkably techy and was able to help me track you down."

My shoulders slump with defeat. I've been so careful to go completely undetected. I haven't talked to anyone from home except for Connie and Odessa, and only ever through the scrambling app. Not necessarily to keep Hayes away, but definitely Carter. Seeing him look at me the way he did in the courtroom only confirmed that he wasn't going to let me go easily.

"Where did I mess up?" I ask, my voice filled with disappointment.

Hayes looks at me sympathetically and replies, "It wasn't anything you did wrong. Lincoln just has a gift for finding people, especially those who don't want to be found. The flight you took to Portland. He got the license plate number off the car that picked you up."

I let out a resigned sigh. I'd be a lot more frustrated if it were anyone but Hayes here. The second I saw him, every single feeling I had shoved down came rushing back.

"So, Iraq? That's where you were?" I still hadn't asked Connie, too afraid to even know.

I don't miss the hint of sadness that clouds him when he asks, "You didn't know?"

"I didn't want to. It was all too hard."

He nods, the hurt evident. "Yeah, we spent a *long* eighteen months there."

"Right. Wait, I have something for you." I reach into my purse and pull out his mint tin, sliding it across the table. "I am so sorry that you didn't have that with you. Carter... He had it. By the time I found it, you were already gone and your mom said she wouldn't be able to send it to you. She thought I could use some of its 'good-luck' juju."

His hand reaches out and our fingers brush while he pulls it back to him. He stares at it like he can't believe it's really in front of him. He swallows hard once before looking at me with misty eyes. "Did you open it?"

I shake my head. "No, to be honest, I could barely look at it."

He pockets it and then looks back toward me. When he doesn't say anything else, I try to fill the silence. "So, how long are you here for? Are you still on leave or is this a long weekend?"

His index finger rubs against his bottom lip before he mumbles. "I got out."

My heart skips a beat at his words. A mix of emotions washes over me—relief, sadness, but mostly guilt that he's given up the thing he loves the most to come find me.

"Hayes... You didn't have to do that for me."

He shakes his head and swallows hard. "My contract was up. I couldn't willingly sign on for more." *Okay, maybe he's not doing it for me?* I feel like I can't get a read on him anymore.

"What about Drew?" I can't even begin to imagine how upset Drew is with me. Running away and hiding. We were raised to be fighters, and the first sign of trouble has me moving across the country and concealing myself from the entire world.

"He's still in. He had already signed another contract while we were deployed. I was dragging my feet, and I hadn't even known why at the time."

My brows draw together as I stare at my plate of food that I haven't touched since he got here.

"Anyway, he was moved to a different team and is going back out again soon." *Another deployment. Color me surprised.* There is an endless cycle of training and deployments for these guys. The only constant for them is that they are always on the move.

I bite the edge of my nail, trying to process the information.

"So, you left the Navy, and now you're here, looking for me? To apologize?" I asked, my voice tinged with disbelief.

He nods solemnly, his eyes never leaving mine. "Yeah. You thought once I knew the whole story, I wouldn't be here..? On my hands and knees, begging for you to forgive me? For you to give me another chance?"

Thank the good lord. Tears well in my eyes. "You couldn't have led with that?" Grabbing my napkin, I dab at my eyes while trying to blink away the tears.

Sandra chooses that moment to pop back over with Hayes' food and set it down. "Anything else, you two?"

I shake my head and avoid eye contact with both of them. I need a minute to compose myself. A minute to figure out how, even after all this time, Hayes still has me wrapped around his stupid finger.

"Thank you. It looks great." Hayes responds in his typical chivalrous-sounding way.

She leaves, but Hayes hasn't moved an inch. I can feel his gaze burning holes into me, but I stare at the same spot on my plate.

"Sunshine. You okay?" His gruff voice comes out, sounding pained.

I look up into those brown eyes and almost lose it again. "Dammit, Hayes. You can't just waltz in here and say all the right things, looking the way you do!" I should be making him suffer. I thought I'd want him to suffer. Make him beg a little, do a little dance, or something. But, no. All I want to do is drag him back to my house and never let him out of my sight again.

His returning grin sends all the butterflies in my stomach fluttering. "I've been driving for the last seventeen hours. I was in no way, shape, or form prepared to see you here," he says, his voice filled with genuine surprise. There's exhaustion in his eyes and weariness etched into every line on his face, but he's still as attractive as he's always been.

"I'm so sorry, Char. I shouldn't have left you that way. I should've listened to what you were saying instead of letting my emotions control me. I don't know if I will ever be able to forgive myself, or if you'll ever be able to forgive me, but I need you to know how sorry I am."

The last of my resolve snaps, just like I knew it would. I can tell the guilt has been eating him alive since he found out.

I reach across the table and grab his hand, intertwining our fingers together. "No, you shouldn't have. But I also shouldn't have had a crazy stalker break into my apartment. This isn't your fault. My leaving South Carolina wasn't your fault either. I needed to be on my own to know I could make it."

His head nods, but I can tell he isn't ready to believe that yet. "What made you choose here?"

Smiling, I squeeze his hand. "The mountains. This town. The people. I love it here. I've made this place home."

The furrow of his eyebrows and lips pressed thin is a guarantee he doesn't like that answer. He was probably hoping to whisk me back to South Carolina.

"Does that mean you won't leave with me?" *Called it.*

I shake my head. "I don't want to leave Three Sisters."

I watch as his shoulders droop low and he hangs his head.

"But you're more than welcome to stay."

His gaze snaps to mine as he gives me one of those huge, knock-me-on-my-ass smiles.

Chapter Twenty-Five

Charlie

I woke up to a very large body wrapped around my entire body. A thumb lightly grazes across my stomach as the rest of his fingers sprawl out. I'm in my own Hayes cocoon that I never want to get out of.

His breathing is even, but I know he's awake. Moving my butt closer into him and wiggling, his thumb stops moving and he lets out a small chuckle.

"Good morning, Sunshine."

I grin into his other arm and roll over with a pouty face. "You fell asleep on me."

He nods as he scans my face, like he's trying to memorize every detail. "I did. You wouldn't let me shower with you, and the second my head hit the pillow and I knew I had you back, it was lights out."

"I had things to take care of. Surprising a girl like that is romantic and all, but I didn't have any time to prep. My leg hair alone would have rivaled Bigfoot."

Grinning, he tickles my ribs. "I've always wanted to go 'Squatch hunting. Now, I've got my very own."

"Har har. When you got back from the first deployment, I had spent days waxing, tweezing, and pampering. Guess you get what you get this time."

He kisses me with a long, slow kiss. "You're perfect. Seeing you yesterday almost took my breath away. You've only gotten more beautiful."

"I love you." It's the first time I've said it since he's been back. I'm done beating around the bush.

His hand engulfs my cheek as he kisses me. "Music to my fucking ears. I love you so much, Charlie. Not a day went by that I didn't love you. Even when I was pissed at you, my heart still only wanted you."

"So there wasn't anyone else?" Not sure why I'm trying to ruin the moment, but with every other card on the table, we might as well throw this one out too.

He shakes his head and laughs. "Hell no. Even if there were options, I wouldn't have wanted to or been able to."

A sigh of relief pops out and my shoulders instantly feel lighter.

"How 'bout you?" The hesitancy in his voice is almost cute. For a split second, I think about teasing him but I'm not sure he could handle that right now.

"Nope. Celibacy was the easiest part of the entire nineteen months."

He laughs, "Same."

"Guess we have a lot to make up for then."

His returning smirk is enough to send a shiver down my spine. "Oh, we definitely do."

His kiss can only be described as feral. The man devours my mouth, pressing his body into mine as he takes control. In a blink, he has my bralette and shorts thrown across the room. The assertive Hayes I missed is officially back. Controlling in the best way, sexy as hell, and sporting a confidence that is irresistible.

We spend the rest of the day making up for lost time.

It isn't until the evening that I realize I haven't checked my phone or even thought about the outside world. Hayes has a way of consuming my attention completely, and I'm not complaining one bit. I should, however, call Drew and explain my side of things and then check in with Olivia. She texted me last night and told me that Dan told her all about the diner run-in. Drew takes priority, though; I've been shutting out my brother for far too long.

Hayes has been softly snoring for a few minutes, so I go in search of my phone.

Finding it, I walk out to the porch and sit on the steps.

The phone rings and rings, and right when I'm about to give up hope, he answers.

"Hello?"

"Hey, big brother—" I try to sound casual, but my voice cracks with emotion.

"Fucking hell, Charlotte." There isn't an ounce of anger in his voice, only concern.

"Heard you've been looking for me?" I try to joke but it comes out weak.

I know that he knows where I am. Hayes told me he called him last night while he was following me out to my house.

"Yeah, Hayes called me. Shit, Charlie. I'm so damn sorry." His tone brings tears to my eyes instantly. He sounds as heartbroken as I felt. "I'm an asshole for brushing you off like that. You deserved more from me."

"You're right, I did. From both of you. However, you can both stop blaming yourselves for my running away. That was all on me; I needed to get as far away from South Carolina as I could. I was terrified of Carter getting out; terrified he wouldn't let it go; terrified he'd only escalate the situation."

"I don't blame you. I should've been there to protect you."

"You couldn't have been there, and you know it. The only person to blame is the one who did the stalking. Carter isn't just crazy; he's dangerous. There isn't anything you or any of us could've done differently."

"That doesn't make me feel any better."

"Me either, but you talking to me wouldn't have changed anything. You and Hayes would have lost your shit and either gotten kicked out of the Navy or killed because you were distracted."

"Probably right. Hayes would have come unglued at the seams, not being able to protect you. Thought he was going to go insane when he couldn't find you."

"Yeah, he mentioned that. So we're all good now? I'll stop hiding in plain sight and you'll stop guilt tripping yourself."

"We're good. I'm glad you two worked it out. He's been a miserable asshole for the last couple of years. Yesterday was the first time I heard him genuinely laugh since before everything happened. He loves the hell out of you, Charlie."

"I love him, too. That never changed. I was only waiting for y'all to get back and come to your senses."

He sighs, but he doesn't deny it. "You're going to move back home, right?"

"This is my home. I love it here. I work for a woman named Olivia, and she's the best—"

He cuts me off. "Charlie, are you serious? You just told me you were done hiding up there!"

Scoffing, I go right into defending myself. "It's not hiding now that you know where I am! I have family, friends, a career!"

"Family? We're your family.." I lose all steam at the sound of his voice breaking with sadness.

"Yeah, Drew. You are and you always will be. But I love these people like family as well."

"Okay. I don't know what to say here, Char."

"Me either. I know things will be weird for a while, but I hated not talking to you. Let's just see how things go for now."

He agreed and after thirty more minutes of catching up, we ended the call with promises to start talking more. Actually, he made me promise I'd text him every day and if I didn't, he'd kick my ass. *Siblings.*

The next call is to Olivia; she answers on the second ring with a squeal. "Tell me everything! I heard he carried you out of SnowPeak over his shoulder, fireman style. Then again, I also heard you slapped him across the face."

I laugh, setting the town gossip straight. "It wasn't quite like that, but it was definitely eventful. Dan cuffing him will be forever ingrained in my memory."

Olivia listens eagerly as I recount the whole story. From when I first saw him sliding into the booth, looking every bit as sexy as I remembered him. To him falling asleep in my bed while I tried to make myself presentable. Looking back, I probably shouldn't have cared as much, considering Hayes has never once cared about stuff like that. I think I just needed the time to wrap my head around everything happening.

"Does this mean we forgive him?"

I chuckle at her use of "we." "Yes. He asked me to move back to South Carolina with him."

I hear her gasp through the phone, but she doesn't say anything.

"Don't worry, I told him no."

"Dammit, Charlie. You scared me! So, do you think he'll stay?" *Million dollar question.*

"I don't know. I hope so." Thinking about him leaving again makes my heart physically ache. I know that I can survive without him, but I don't want to. Nor do I want to leave Three Sisters.

My heart belongs here.

Hopefully, his decides it does too.

Chapter Twenty-Six

Charlie

Saturday, January 5.

Hand in hand, I half-dragged Hayes into the Cascadia Winter Festival. Every year, the town throws a winter festival, and it's one of my favorite events. There are booths with baked goods, food carts, and local beers for sale everywhere. Kids games, hand-carved ice sculptures, and live music fill the streets. My favorite part is the skijoring, though. Our version of a snow rodeo, where skiers are pulled behind horses competing for the fastest time. It's always chaos, but the participants have a good time and don't take it too seriously, at least.

I can't wait for Hayes to meet Olivia, Ben, and Ellie. Along with the rest of Three Sisters. These people welcomed me from the start, embracing me as part of their community. I knew they would do the same for Hayes. As we walked through the festival, I pointed out familiar faces and introduced him to everyone I knew. Despite the frigid air, the sense of belonging and warmth were evident, making me even more excited for Hayes to experience it all.

"Everyone here loves you." He comments with a smile after the tenth person has introduced themselves.

"Looks like they love you too." He's the new hot commodity, and everyone is falling over themselves to meet him. Especially the women. They all stare at him like he's a piece of meat for the grabbing.

He wraps his free arm around me, pulling me in closer. "Forgot how much I like that little jealous streak."

Honestly, I almost forgot I had a jealous streak; however, it was quite severe back then. I was young and willing to throw down with anyone to assert my dominance. Hard not to when you're dating a guy who looks like Hayes and women have no shame.

"Remember the time that woman gave you her number in front of me?"

He chuckles as we walk. "You mean when I had to physically hold you back from punching her in the face?"

"Yep. Still wish you would've let me."

"And ruin our trip to the Bahamas? No way. I had you in a bikini with unlimited drinks. No way was I giving that up to have to bail you out of jail."

We walk around a bit more, and finally I spot Olivia and the rest of the family schmoozing it up at the Cascadia Sheriff booth. Dan is holding Ellie and chatting with another local, while Olivia smiles at everything he says. She's told me before how much she hates these things, but looking at her, you'd never be able to tell. She shines just as brightly as Dan does, and she does it all for him. His goal is to eventually run for Sheriff once his dad retires. A lot of that is pleasing the town, and Dan is the ultimate people pleaser. Olivia does everything with a smile, and if it weren't for the exhaustion hidden behind her eyes, I'd never know she was only doing it to be the dutiful wife.

Olivia sees us, and her eyes widen a fracture before a real smile lights up her face and she excuses herself and Ben.

"Hi! It's so nice to officially meet you. I am so sorry that I had to lie to you the other day." She says it with a sheepish grin.

Hayes chuckles. "Don't worry about it. I'm glad you were looking out for my girl." *Swoon.*

Ben looks up at Hayes and then back to his mom, confusion written all over his four year old little face. "Mom, lying's bad."

Olivia smiles easily, letting it roll off her shoulders. "This is one of those gray areas, buddy. Most of the time, lying is bad. But sometimes we have to make tough choices to help the people we care about."

Hayes squats so that he's on Ben's level. "Your mom's right. I'm glad she didn't tell me the truth, because she did it to keep Charlie safe.

I hear a small laugh starting to escape Olivia. "Yep, and my introduction wasn't even as bad as your dad's. Did you know that when he first saw Hayes, he tried to arrest him?"

Ben's little eyes go wide. "You?! But you're huge!"

Dan walks over to give Ellie to Olivia and laughs upon hearing the rest of the conversation. "Hey! He's not *that* big, and I'm a trained professional."

Then he sticks his hand out to shake Hayes hand as Hayes stands back up. "Sorry again about that. I don't normally rip people out of a booth unprovoked."

Chuckling, I say, "It's really a bummer no one got a picture. I can already see the news headline for the Cascadia Gazette, "Lieutenant Dan manhandles Navy SEAL to the ground.""

"Ha, Ha, Char." He gives me a hug and then looks back at Hayes again.

"I know she's got a big brother who's probably already given you the speech, but in case you forgot, don't hurt her again. Or else, I really will manhandle you and throw you in a cell."

My cheeks feel hotter than normal at all this attention, but I'm so grateful for the Turners and all they've done for me. Dan's taken on that big brother role without even blinking. He's got a heart of gold and doesn't even realize he changed my life with the simple action of sending me to my best friend.

Hayes wraps his arm around me and kisses my forehead.

Hayes

Still holding on to Charlie, I look at Dan. "I appreciate you looking out for her when I wasn't. I'm mad as hell that she felt like she had to leave, but I'm glad she found y'all. If there's one good thing to come out of all this, at least it's that."

Dan looks at me, assessing me one more time, and then smiles. "Olivia and I had no doubt that you'd be here groveling the second you found out. Glad to see you proved us right."

"Thanks, man. Appreciate the vote of confidence."

Olivia pats Ellies back while slightly rocking her. "I'm going to walk over to the office and grab her stroller so she can nap."

Charlie smiles and says, "I'll go with you!" Then she kisses my cheek. "Grab a beer for me?"

They walk away, taking Ben with them, and Dan loses all sense of ease—the smile slipping from his face.

"Let's get in line for that beer." He motions toward the beer tent, which has at least thirty people in line.

Nodding, I follow him, unease hitting me like a sixth sense.

"What's up? You look like you're about to tell me you ran over my cat."

His cheeks puff out as he lets a breath out. "We haven't told Charlie yet, because we don't have any proof that it's her stalker but..." My heart rate picking up is the only sign of the panic overtaking my body and I haven't even heard the entirety of

164

what he has to say. The visceral need to want to run away and hide with her hits me hard. *Now I know how Charlie felt.*

"Olivia has received a handful of calls over the last few weeks, from random numbers asking for Charlotte Reynolds. One of them was you, but that's all we know. Every time she's sent me the information, I've tried to trace the calls but they're deadends—burner phones and location scramblers. Olivia did a good job of deflecting but my gut is telling me it isn't a coincidence."

"Fuck. I'll let Detective Paul know. He was the one on the case and might be able to check into more. He's a good guy and seems to care a lot about Charlie and my mom."

"That's a good idea. Mind sending me his info? Not that I hold more weight than you, but I can give him all the details I have."

"Yeah, I'll text you his contact information. I've got a friend who is pretty good at digging as well. He, uh, doesn't exactly go by the book, though."

He lifts his hand in surrender and smirks. "Best to pretend that I didn't hear any of that." His face grows a little more serious when he says, "Do what you need to do to make sure she stays safe."

After we exchange numbers, the guilt of Charlie being unaware starts to fester. "I think we should tell Charlie. It's going to scare the hell out of her, but if she finds out she's being kept in the dark, she will go nuclear."

Dan chuckles. "I agree. We were only keeping it quiet because we didn't have much to go on and we were afraid she would leave again. Now that you're here, I feel a hell of a lot better about her safety."

We both agreed it'd be better to wait until after the festival and let her live in the moment a little longer. This is going to send her on an emotional rollercoaster, but it's better she knows the truth sooner rather than later.

How Charlie stumbled upon such a good family in Oregon is beyond me, but they really are amazing. We spent the rest of the day with them, enjoying the festival and sharing stories about her. Everything they've told me brings a little relief to the guilt I've been feeling. She took an incredibly traumatic event and turned it into an opportunity to become a better version of herself. The tenacity of this woman isn't just admirable; it's awe-inspiring. She created an entire new life here—new family, new friends, new job—and never gave up on me in the process. I don't know where I'll fit in her world anymore or what I'll do for work around here but I'm not about to let that stop me from doing everything I can to be with her.

Being here has only proven what I already knew. I'm madly in love with Charlie, and no matter what, I'll be fighting tooth and nail to give her the life she wants. If that means spending the rest of my life in a small Oregon town, then so be it. For Charlie, I'd live in a tent in the woods.

Chapter Twenty-Seven

Charlie

Saturday, February 16.

Ponderosa Pine Bar and Grill is having its official grand reopening. Ethan bought it about a month after he moved home with baby Jake. Apparently he worked there in high school before he left for college and then on to play in the NFL. Once things settled down with being a single dad to an infant, Ethan started renovating the building and got to work.

Ethan was best friends with Olivia all through grade school, so she's been helping him with the entire renovation and also everything to do with Jake. His parents have also played a pivotal role in helping him with everything, and tonight is the first night we get to celebrate him opening up his new business.

He went all out at this restaurant. It looks like a ski lodge with wood fireplaces, comfortable tables, and cozy lighting. Everything looks like he spent top dollar on it, which, knowing him, I'm sure he did.

We get there a little after the party has started and it's

packed. The whole town showed up to support him and his family. Well, everyone but Maisie. I still haven't figured out what the issue is. After he got home, Maisie ran out of my party and then stopped coming around as much. Olivia tries to keep the friendship up, but Maisie doesn't want anything to do with Ethan; therefore, Olivia by proxy, and me by proxy-proxy. It's not that we were best friends to begin with, but I'm disappointed that I'm guilty by association.

Olivia, Dan, and Levi sit in a corner booth with Luke and Madelyn. Even from a distance, it looks awkward. Levi's normal, jovial self looks like he's trying to hide behind Olivia. I found out at my birthday party that Madelyn consistently tries to make Luke jealous, just to "poke the bear." Luke never reacts and that only makes her try harder. Poor Levi is caught in the crossfire and has no idea how to handle it.

I point toward their table and Hayes' eyes go wide. "Holy shit, she looks just like..."

"Dess?" I finish for him and he grins.

"I know, doppelgängers." They may look exactly alike—blonde, tall, and beautiful—but their personalities are the complete opposite. Madelyn is overly sweet and a little fake, whereas Odessa is headstrong and not afraid to share her opinion.

As we approach the table, Levi sees us first. "Ahh, if it isn't the one that got away! Returning to me, with her one that got away." He trails off in the last part, as if even he is trying to make sense of what he's saying.

Hayes looks between the two of us with a raised eyebrow.

Thank God for Olivia, piping up. "Levi, don't you dare start causing trouble already. She can't be the one who got away if she was never yours to begin with."

He waves his hand, dismissing her logic. "Semantics." Then he narrows his eyes, pretending to assess Hayes.

168

Hayes glances around the table, trying to figure out what the hell is going on with Levi's cryptic behavior.

Luke chuckles from behind his beer and Dan rolls his eyes. The whole interaction may have lasted five seconds of awkward silence, but finally Levi smirked and nodded his approval.

"You'll do. I was worried she was pining over some loser."

I scoff at Levi. "Like you have any say, considering your track record with relationships."

Levi just shrugs, unfazed by my comment. "Nah, you can't have a track record if you don't have any relationships."

Hayes chuckles and extends his hand. "Nice to meet you. Levi was it?"

Levi grins back and shakes his hand. "Yep. That's Luke and Madelyn, and I'm sure you know Dan and Liv."

I watch as Hayes tries to greet Luke and Madelyn, but Madelyn looks caught in a daze as she stares at Hayes. Luke nudges her with his elbow, snapping her out of it and she smiles coyly. "Nice to meet you too."

Hayes clears his throat, breaking the awkward silence. "So, this place is pretty cool. Can't believe y'all are friends with Ethan Flacco."

Dan nods. "Big Vikings fan?"

Hayes shakes his head. "Nah, but a guy I worked with was. He's going to lose his shit when he finds out I'm at his restaurant."

Olivia starts smiling from her little corner and I know I'm about to be in trouble.

"Don't you even go there, Olivia Turner." I warn.

"Go where?" Hayes looks between the two of us.

Dan smiles as big as Olivia does, clearly knowing what we are both thinking. "Charlie thought we hired Ethan as a stripper for her birthday."

My face heats up to an embarrassing shade of red. *Asshole.*

"You thought they hired one of the greatest quarterbacks in NFL history to strip for you?"

"No! I didn't know who he was and I was a little drunk when he knocked on Olivia's door."

Maddy giggles. "In her defense, there was a lot of alcohol, and well, he looks like that." She says this while gesturing behind us toward the football god.

I turn to see Ethan walking to our table, and the embarrassment only intensifies.

"Hey, everyone! Thanks for coming." He looks to Hayes and extends his hand, "Ethan Flacco."

Hayes smirks, "Hayes Carrington. Heard you're the one to call if we need a stripper."

"Hayes!" I smack him in the chest, only causing him to laugh harder."

Ethan's eyes go slightly wide and then he's laughing with everyone else. "I'll admit, no one has ever opened the door and immediately thought I was an exotic dancer before. But I took it as a compliment." Thankfully, I've spent enough time with Ethan that this story isn't as embarrassing as it once was.

Deciding to just roll with it, I slide into the seat next to Levi. "Well, at least we know if this fancy restaurant doesn't make it, you can audition for Magic Mike."

Hayes grins and sits next to me. "This place is awesome. You did a good job here. Charlie told me y'all renovated the whole building."

Ethan nods, his entire face lighting up. "Thanks, man. Yeah, my dad and brothers own a construction company so I used them for a lot of free labor."

"I agree. Ethan, this place is exactly what Three Sisters needed. You outdid yourself." Dan raised his glass for a toast.

Olivia's eyes go a little misty but she holds up her glass too. "We're so glad you're back."

Ethan's face turns three shades of red but he grins back. "Happy to be home."

Our server comes over and we both order a drink and some food. When she excuses herself to go put the order in, Luke and Levi both start grilling Hayes. Slightly surprising, considering Dan is usually the one who's always in Lieutenant mode.

Levi starts off, "You planning on stayin' here for a while?"

I reach down and place my hand on Hayes thigh, hoping I can give some reassurance.

Hayes takes all the questions with ease. "As long as Charlie will let me. I'm a handful of terms away from finishing my bachelor's degree—business management. I have a meeting with OSU Cascades to see what will transfer from what I was doing online while overseas."

Luke nods his head. "You sure you're not looking for a job at the department? Someone with your skills and history could be an asset."

Hayes chuckles. "Thought about it, but I'm leaning more toward the desk route right now. I missed out on a lot of stuff— birthdays and holidays. I don't want to be in a position for that again."

I squeezed his thigh while grinning at him. We've had a lot of in depth talks about our future over the last few months. We both agreed we want to try to have normal, nine-to-five jobs that we aren't risking our lives in. I think Hayes needs to get a little normalcy back in his life so that he can heal. He's down-played all the traumatic events he had while he was deployed but I'm afraid those will resurface in unhealthy ways.

All of the guys nodded and lifted their beers to him for that. None of them are immune to the hardships that being a first responder has. They've all had to put their work first and their families second at points in their careers. Olivia picked up her water and took a small sip, avoiding eye contact. I already know the heartbreaking thought that she's thinking—even if Dan had the option, he wouldn't change his career.

Luke and Madelyn call it an early night after about an hour. There seemed to be a little tension lingering in the air, but Madelyn ignored it and Luke shut down. I offhandedly asked Olivia if it had anything to do with Hayes and me showing up, but she assured me they were like that before we even got there.

Levi flirted his way through the bar, being Ethan's wingman even though Ethan wanted nothing to do with him. It was actually pretty entertaining to watch Ethan awkwardly avoid any advances toward him. He's been so focused on Jake and the bar that I doubt he's dated since he's been back.

Olivia and Dan danced for most of the night. He looks at her like she's God's gift to earth and she smiles right back at him. I know she has been pretty candid with me about their struggles in the past, but seeing them tonight, it's clear that they have a strong connection.

When they decided to call it a night, we did too. It was fun being out with everyone, but all I wanted to do was go home and be cozy with my man.

<hr>

My phone rings early—too early for a Monday morning, 6 a.m. early.

"It's your mom."

Hayes looks at me with sleepy eyes and says with a yawn, "My mom?"

I don't even answer his rhetorical question.

"Hey, everything okay?" It's 9 a.m. eastern time, but

Connie normally waits a few hours before calling because she knows that.

"Hi, sweetheart. Hayes with you?" Her tone already sounds off and I sit up in bed, putting it on speakerphone.

"He's here; you're on speaker phone."

She lets out a deep breath. "I got a call from Detective Paul. Carter's being released for good behavior next week. It's been about two-and-a half years. He'll be on probation, but I wanted you to know the second I did."

Hayes' entire body shifts from relaxed to predatory mode. His eyes go dark as his body tenses. I can almost see the wheels turning in his mind. I have no doubt that if we weren't across the country, Carter would be mysteriously missing by now.

I gripped his forearm with pleading eyes. I can't lose Hayes again. If he goes searching for Carter, things will get bad.

"Thanks for letting us know. I'll call Detective Paul and see if there's anything we should do." Hayes told me a few weeks ago that they suspected Carter already knew where I was. All that hard work was for nothing. Thankfully, now that Hayes is here, the news doesn't hit me as hard as I thought it would.

"Ok, sweet girl. I pray every day that he learns from this and is reformed."

Hayes scoffs, knowing full well the chances of that are slim. His brows furrowed together as he stared at the phone in my hand. "Mom, you going to be okay? I can have someone come stay with you."

"I'll be fine. Don't you worry about me. All my neighbors look out for each other and keep a good watch."

I can see the worry in Hayes already, but he acquiesces.

We catch up for a few more minutes and then hang up.

Hayes falls back onto his pillow, closing his eyes. The noticeable jaw ticking is the only thing I can see moving on him.

"Do you want to go stay with your mom?" I ask, more worried about how he's feeling than myself at this point.

"And leave you? Absolutely not."

"I'm safe here. Between Dan, Luke, and Levi—"

"No." His tone leaves no room for argument, but that's never stopped me before.

"Hayes, I can tell you're worried about your mom."

His eyes fly open, and he sits up, placing his hand on my jawline.

"No. My mom has more security than you do and I have some friends that can stay with her if he decides to show up. I'm not leaving you again. I *can't* leave you again." The way his voice breaks tugs at every single one of my heart strings.

"Ok, I don't want you to go either."

"Good." His shoulders sag and I kiss him. A long, slow kiss that evolves into something much, much more.

Chapter Twenty-Eight

Hayes

Sunday, April 21.

The Turners are hosting Easter at Zeke's' house this year. Apparently, it's a huge deal, involving a small Easter hunt for the kids and a huge Easter hunt for the adults. The invite said to bring your own ATV, binoculars, and rope. I have no idea what that means, but it sounds like a training mission and I'm all in.

I ended up going into Bend and buying a side-by-side so that Charlie and I could roll in style. Not my smartest financial move, considering I'm technically unemployed but I saved more than enough from my time in the Navy and I haven't touched the decent-sized inheritance my grandparents left for me. Well, except to buy Charlie that ring a few years ago. The ring that is still in my dad's mint tin—sitting on top of our dresser. I'd give it to her right this second if I thought the timing was right. It's not, though; Carter is still a worry on her mind and things don't feel as settled as they should.

We arrived early to help set up and it was chaos already. Charlie jumped into action, helping Olivia, and I volunteered to be on kid duty so the other adults could "hide" the kids eggs and finish prepping the food.

Zeke spent a week hiding the adult's eggs and there's an entire system of rankings. All eggs are point-based; the person with the most points wins the title of Easter MVP and a $300 gift card to Buckaroo Bills, the only clothing store in town besides the Alpaca one. A clothing gift card isn't something I'd normally be excited about, but I could use a wardrobe overhaul to fit in this town. It's all cowboy boots and wranglers around here. Even Charlie seems to be dressing a little more country than she ever has before.

The kids and I hung out in the living room, building tower after tower with Magnatiles. Ben and I would build it high so that Ellie could knock it over. Over and over again. Ben randomly started calling me "Uncle Hayes" and I almost got misty-eyed over it the first time. The two of them have me wrapped around their little fingers, and I've only been here a few months. It's no surprise that Charlie doesn't want to leave.

When it was time for the kids to do their egg hunt, they found every single one in about three minutes. The eggs were mostly just thrown about in the yard; a dozen or so hidden a little harder for Ben but he had no problem spotting them.

Standing next to Zeke, I bumped my shoulder into his and said, "Hope yours is a little more challenging than this one."

"Get ready. Last year, Will brought his canine to track them down. He only beat Charlie by three points."

Charlie's eyes narrow at an SUV pulling in. "This year, I brought a Navy SEAL, though."

Zeke let out a loud, boisterous laugh. "Can't wait to tell Will that." He starts walking toward the SUV as a shorter guy with a bloodhound gets out. How Charlie thinks I can compete with a trained bloodhound is beyond me, but I'm not going to let her know that. I've got a little showing off I still need to do.

Thirty minutes later, Zeke is going over the rules. "Alright, everyone! Listen up. You have two hours! The rules are: no cheating, violence, or stealing. Let's keep it friendly and fair. Golden eggs are worth 10 points; camouflaged eggs are worth 5; all other colors are worth 1 point. There are a total of 300 eggs out there. We're here to have a good time and test our skills, not to cause any trouble." He pauses, scanning the group as a warning. I swear he eyes Charlie just a little longer than the rest. "Remember, this is just a friendly competition. Let's show some sportsmanship and respect for each other. Also, don't forget to check yourself for ticks. Scavenger on!"

Charlie glares at Will, already forgetting all about the "friendly" part of the competition.

"Hey, Will! You teach that old dog any new tricks?"

Will grins and confidently asks, "Did you?" while gesturing at me. *Doesn't even know the grave he just dug for himself.*

"Let's go, Sunshine." I pull her toward the side-by-side, ready to set our game plan and show her everything I bought.

I have it loaded with the tools Zeke recommended as well as ones that I thought could be helpful—a brush axe, two extendable grabbing tools that have different ends for scooping, a topographical map, flashlights, rope, and a knife.

Charlie said the eggs are often found in trees or buried under brush, and very few are hidden in plain sight.

Our competition is mostly Search and Rescue members and anyone else that volunteers on their small force, but there's a lot of people here. A lot of trained professionals whose sole job revolves around looking for hidden things.

"Last year, I went all the way out to the edge of the property and then worked my way in. I stopped for the small ones if they were easy to reach but the big ones were my priority. Those golden eggs are the hardest to find and get to, but worth it."

I nod, and when Zeke shouts go, we hop in and start driving.

Charlie is incredible at this, spotting eggs in places that I'd never even thought to look for. I thought two hours would be plenty of time, but when the countdown starts ticking, the pressure hits. We left the side-by-side at the edge of the property and have been strategically making our way back to the finish line.

Charlie is ravenous to find more, practically foaming at the mouth. I've only found a few handfuls, but they've all been golden or camouflaged. Charlie has found dozens, of all colors. She even scurried up a tree like a squirrel when the poles wouldn't reach it.

I'm thoroughly impressed... And a little scared.

Finally, Zeke calls a three-minute warning and we all sprint toward the finish line, carrying bags of plastic eggs. Adults of all shapes and sizes shove each other like children to make sure they get there.

While Charlie hovers over Zeke and Elise, counting the eggs, I walk over to stand by Dan and Luke.

"That was awesome. Brought back some of the good training memories. The ones that weren't so serious and more about team bonding than anything else."

Dan laughs and hands me a beer. "Yeah, Pop has always gone all out. It's good training for the team and they still get to have fun. I can't believe how many you two found, though."

"Have you met Charlie? Once she loses at something, she's determined for the next round."

"Learned that during a lively game of Uno. Thought she was going to kick my ass when I put down a 'draw 4.'"

I chuckle back. "Been there before."

"How's she holding up since the release?"

"Better than me. I'm seeing shadows everywhere I look." I don't normally vent to people I've only known for a short amount of time. However, Dan is one of those guys who's easy to talk to.

He takes a sip of his beer and then asks, "You worried he's going to come all the way out here?"

"I don't know. I want to say no. It seems crazy to think that he'd try to get across the country. But..."

"But it's crazy to think that she had a stalker to begin with."

"Exactly. My gut is telling me this isn't over."

Dan nods and sighs, "Mine too. I called Detective Paul after you gave me his number at the Winter Festival. He thinks Carter is smarmy and arrogant, and his gut is telling him the same thing as ours. Carter's still obsessed with Charlie. Guy got a sleeve of white roses tattooed on him in prison."

"Fuck." I scrub my hand down my face.

He claps me on the shoulder. "I'm glad she has you. I was worried, based on your history, but I can tell you're one of the good ones."

"Thanks, Dan. Feel the same about you. All of you, really. I'll always be thankful that this town hid my girl so well. But I'll forever be indebted to *you* for sending her to Liv. Without her, I don't think she would've stayed and flourished the way she did."

"Those two are kindred spirits. They both helped each other in a way that you and I couldn't."

I nodded in response. The two of them are inseparable. They work together every day, hang out on weekends, and text when they aren't together. They act like they've known each other their entire lives—sisters more than friends.

I know Drew holds some resentment toward them for hiding her, but I don't look at it that way. They did what we should have—took care of her and supported her during a time she felt scared and abandoned. If it ever came down to it, I'd do everything in my power to repay both Dan and Olivia for all they've done for Charlie.

Chapter Twenty-Nine

Charlie

Friday, August 30.

Olivia and I have been working non-stop all day. She's been on the phone, handling one crisis after another, while I try to keep up with our normal workload. Both of us ended up eating lunch at our desk, working straight through it. Fridays can be a mess sometimes. Everyone knows our office is closed on the weekends and decides to call with whatever issue they think can't wait until Monday.

I try not to laugh as she animatedly talks to Jared, who owns the landscape company we use. She's been trying to convince him to switch their route so that our tenant, Mrs. Lentfer, doesn't have her meditation interrupted anymore. Mrs. Lentfer calls every Friday, like clockwork, complaining about the noise. It's exhausting to listen to, and finally, Olivia couldn't deal anymore and decided to beg Jared to switch her timeframe.

She hangs up the phone and flops back in her chair. "All the tenants do is bitch. Every one of them has a problem."

I chuckle back. "That's why you get paid the big bucks."

She sighs. "Fine. You're right. Want to ride with me to Maisie's? I need some caffeine to survive this afternoon crash."

"Absolutely. Everything still super weird with all that?"

"Yup. I'm going to keep trying, though. Let her know my friendship is still there when she's ready."

The drive to Maisie's coffee hut isn't far, but it is on the other side of town. Olivia pulls in behind a line that is three cars deep. When we are next in line, I look up to see a giant bouquet of white roses on the ledge of the window.

Goosebumps erupt along my skin, just like they always do. The sight of the flowers alone has me involuntarily cringing but I swear I've been seeing them more often. It seems like every store in Three Sisters is boasting cryptic bouquets.

Olivia lets out a small gasp when she sees them. Quietly, almost a whisper, she says, "What the fuck?"

We stay silent until it's our turn. Maisie greets us with a warm smile and is overly friendly as always.

"What can I get you for you ladies?"

I shake my head, suddenly not able to stomach anything. Olivia orders some treats, as well as an iced coffee for her and an iced green tea for me. She gives me a sympathetic smile and says, "In case you change your mind."

"Here you go!" Maisie smiles at us, but it looks forced. Once again reminding me, our friend has pulled so far away that she has to fake a smile around us.

"Thanks, Mais. Hey, where'd the flowers come from? It seems like they're all over town."

Maisie grins back, completely unaware of the unease we are feeling. "Not sure. Someone delivered them yesterday, no note or anything."

My vision begins tunneling as I stare at my shaking heads. I don't even hear what Olivia says back. I completely zoned out the drive back to the office, trying not to hyperventilate in my seat from a panic attack. It isn't until my door is suddenly yanked open that I snap out of it.

"Sunshine." I look to Hayes as the first tears spill over.

"He's here!" I wail, sounding like an upset teenager.

Hayes pulls me into his arms. "He isn't here. He's trying to fuck with us. I talked to his probation officer, and he saw him this morning. In South Carolina."

That should make me feel better, but it doesn't. Carter is always one step ahead of us. Skirting by and laying low until he strikes.

"What is this? A sick game of cat and mouse? Am I some kind of prey?"

Hayes shakes his head and holds my head against his chest. "I don't know. But if it is, he's forgetting one thing. I'm the Golden Eagle here. Apex predator, baby, I have no problem hunting his ass down. Talons out."

A small laugh bubbles out and I hold onto him tighter. Having Hayes here, reassuring me, is everything I wanted when all of this first started. He's strong enough to hold us both up, and he still manages to make me laugh. He calls me his sunshine, but it's the same when I think about him. He's the light in my dark times.

Dan pulls into the office parking lot in his cruiser. Olivia meets him at his door and quietly explains everything she knows. I watch as he nods, a serious look masking the concern I know is there.

He gives her a hug, holding her like Hayes is holding me. The universal masculine hug of reassurance that lets us know they're here to fix all our problems.

Pulling away from Hayes, I lace my fingers through his as we walk over to them.

"Hey, Char. We've got everyone who is free checking in

with the businesses that have flowers. All we know right now is that they've come on different days and none of them have had any notes."

My eyebrows naturally rise. "That didn't take long. It's been like fifteen minutes."

He tries to smile, but ends up just nodding instead. "Small town. With a lot of people that care about you."

"What do we do now? Sit around and wait for more calls? More flower deliveries?" Frustration radiates out of Hayes.

Dan huffs out a breath of air and then rubs the back of his neck. "I don't know, Hayes. I need to talk to my dad. See what he wants us all to do. I think it's safe to say that for now, Charlie doesn't go anywhere alone."

I nod my head. I thought I'd be the tough girl who said she didn't need a babysitter, but right now, that isn't me. I'll take five armed babysitters, an armored car, and a flame thrower. I don't know if it was luck or skill that brought Carter down the first time, but I'm not taking any chances.

Chapter Thirty

Charlie

My feet unconsciously shift back and forth from nerves as I stand in the deli, waiting for the order I called in thirty minutes ago. I was hoping it would be done already, but it's unusually busy today and looks understaffed. Hayes is going to be livid if he finds out I ran across the street by myself, but I wasn't prepared for the line of people out the door and Olivia was on the phone. I'm back to being a prisoner of the fear that is Carter and I'm trying not to let it completely cripple me.

Officially, one week has passed since the flower debacle and I keep seeing them pop up every now and then. Most of the town knows what's going on, though, and has been throwing them away. There's still no proof that Carter has been sending them, but Detective Paul assures me every day that he is keeping a close eye on the situation. It's a blessing to know that he cares so much and is taking this just as seriously as we are.

Hayes has barely left my side for the last week, to the point where I have to convince him to leave me alone so that I can use the bathroom by myself. It took thirty minutes for me to convince him to go have some guy time, but he acquiesced when I told him guns and ammo would be involved and I wouldn't leave Olivia's side. *Whoops.* At least I know that he's spending the afternoon blowing off steam, as he knows best. Hopefully he comes home in a better mood because the brooding is only adding to my anxiety.

Lost in thought, daydreaming about Hayes, I feel a hand reach out and touch my elbow, causing me to nearly jump out of my skin.

"Shoot! Sorry, Charlie!" Camilla looks at me with eyes full of remorse and the initial panic I felt dissipates. Camilla was one of the first people I met when I moved here and is the least threatening person in the entire town.

"Not your fault at all! I was distracted and evidently very jumpy."

She giggles and nods. "Sounds like you have a right to be. The flowers? What the hell?"

My eyes roll as I shake my head. "It's insane. This guy is completely insane."

"Yeah, that's putting it nicely. The entire town is ready to grab their pitchforks and storm to South Carolina, though. You're loved here, girl. If you need anything, please let us know." She says it with such sincerity that I can't help but feel loved.

"Thank you. I appreciate everyone here so much." I give her a hug and pull back. "What's new with you? Dating anyone?"

"Ugh. No. I can't even think about that right now. We just heard from our landlord that they're selling our building. My parents are freaking out. We've been renting from them for years, and they just sprung it on us. If they hadn't just invested so much into the vineyard next to our farm, it wouldn't be a problem."

"You're kidding me?! I'll talk to Olivia and see what she

thinks." Olivia knows more about the town than the mayor does. She's friends with everyone and they love her. I'm honestly surprised she doesn't know about this yet. The woman has eyes and ears everywhere, it seems.

Camilla and I spend another ten minutes talking about the property before my food is ready and I say goodbye. It already sounds like an incredible investment. The building is right on Main Street, the sellers aren't looking to make a ton of money, and we already know and trust the tenants.

"Olivia!" I yell while running up the stairs of the office. "OLIVIA!" By the time I make it to the top of the stairs, she's stepping out of our office, panic written all over her face at my screaming. *Oops. The one time I went anywhere alone and now I'm screaming for her.*

"It's good! I'm good." I speak breathlessly. In hindsight, running and yelling probably wasn't my smartest idea.

Her shoulders visibly relax. "What's going on?"

"I just ran into Camilla at the deli. She told me the building they're leasing is about to go up for sale. Apparently, the owners are from California and need to liquidate a bunch of their assets. She only knows because they just called her. They can't buy it because they just bought the vineyard."

Olivia smirks at me and sings, "Someone's caught the investor bug." She laughs and then says, "Seriously, you've brought me more property listings than my real estate agent."

I grin back at her, full of pride. "So you want to look at it? It would be perfect for your portfolio!"

She purses her lips and then shakes her head. "Nah."

Shock rocks through me that she isn't interested. Olivia has always been involved in investing in the town. She hates when outsiders buy up all the property just to rent it out, especially because they always jack up the prices.

"Why the hell not? Do you think it'll be overpriced?"

She shrugs. "I'm not worried about that. I don't have enough time to handle any more properties right now. Not until I hire a new "you" and then give you the promotion you deserve, anyway."

My shoulders fall as I say, "Oh." Then it hits me, "Wait, what?"

She grins from ear to ear. "I want you to be my COO. You can make the small decisions and report to me on the big stuff, but I trust you. You're getting an assistant, a raise, and an actual title."

My jaw drops further with each word she says, completely in disbelief. "Me? You want to make me your COO?"

"Yep. You've earned it!"

A very unladylike squeal screeches out of me as I do a small happy dance.

Olivia laughs and gives me a hug. "I was planning on sitting you down and telling you all business-like, but this was way more fun!"

"I have to call Hayes!" He's with Dan, Luke, and Levi at the shooting range, having guy time. The four of them have become quite the man tribe.

Hayes answers in the first ring, "Hey, Sunshine."

"Guess what?! You're talking to the new COO of Cascades Property Management! And I'm getting an assistant!" I squeal into the phone again, not able to hide my excitement. I went from an unknown assistant to the COO of a huge company.

"No shit? Congratulations, beautiful!"

"Thanks, babe! I'll let you get back to shoot'n guns. I love you!"

Chapter Thirty-One

Hayes

"Love you too. Let's celebrate tonight!"

Charlie ends the call and I grin at my phone before putting it back in my pocket. She's earned that promotion and it's nice to see that she's being recognized for it. I'm more excited that she's so happy, though. The last few months have been tumultuous at best, always waiting for the next sign of Carter.

"What's up with Charlie?" Levi asks, before handing back the Glock G19 pistol he was checking out. We've been at the shooting range most of the afternoon, celebrating my new concealed handgun license. After spending 18 months with a gun on me at all times, I felt naked without one. I was itching to get my CHL from the minute I moved here. Part of that required me to have a valid Oregon driver's license. That was the easy part; the hard part was getting my CHL appointment. I didn't want to pull any strings with Zeke, but now, looking back, I should have. Due to the backlog, it took me an additional six months to get my CHL. Thankfully, as of yesterday, I can finally carry my Sig around again.

Dan smirks at me. "Let me guess? Big promotion?"

Levi looks between the two of us and I nod. "Yep, she's got an official title and everything."

"Hell yeah. Olivia's business has been thriving now that she's not doing it all by herself. No offense, D."

Dan chuckles. "None taken. Liv was a rock star before but now she's unstoppable. The two of them are going to own the entire town by the time they're done."

"Good plan. I could use an early retirement."

"Ha. You and I, both."

From the other side of me, Luke asks, "You talk to your friend at all? See if he can confirm it was Carter that's been sending the flowers in town."

"He did a little sniffing around. Carter is apparently very good at covering his tracks, but it's looking like the flowers were from him. Same with the phone calls. Problem is, we can't exactly prove it the legal way. Detective Paul is aware of everything, but it's still in limbo without a warrant. A small town receiving flower bouquets isn't exactly reason enough to go to a judge. The guy's grandma died while he was in prison, too. Left him with a shit ton of money, a fancy house, and a private jet."

I watch as Levi taps his fingers on the glass case, clearly wanting to say something but keeping his mouth shut.

"Say what ya need to say, Levi. You're makin' me nervous."

"Even though I'm the son of the Sheriff, I'm a firm believer that the legal way isn't always the best route to go."

Dan rolls his eyes. "Always a hothead."

Levi shrugs. "Just hope the asshole gets what's coming to him. That's all." It's the first time I'm starting to see another side of Levi. The more I'm around him, the more he reminds me of Everett. Always making a joke, but ready to kick someone's ass the second they cross a line.

I look him dead in the eye and nod once, letting him know I

knew exactly what he meant. Levi just moved up a few points in my book. The always goofy one, ready to be the next vigilante with me.

If he wasn't affecting our day-to-day lives so much, I may be able to let Carter's bullshit go and wait for his inevitable slip up. However, he's messing with Charlie's head to the point where she's scared of her shadow. I'm tired of it all. Tired of her being scared to answer her cell phone. Tired of the nightmares she has. Tired of how much of our lives are consumed by this asshole.

With every unknown call she gets, my patience wears thin. I'm teetering on the edge of hunting this asshole down once and for all. It's a good thing Charlie picked one of the furthest states away from South Carolina, putting an entire country between us. My mind has already thought of a hundred ways I could make him disappear and I'm not above doing any of them. After all, what's one more scar on my already calloused heart?

Chapter Thirty-Two

Hayes

Tuesday, October 1.

The calls haven't stopped coming, but the town has at least taken care of the flower deliveries. All of the locals know by now that if they receive any white roses, they need to call Zeke and report them before immediately throwing them away. We know Carter is choosing out-of-town florists to deliver them and not leaving a paper trail. I don't know what his endgame is, but each delivery is only enraging the town. They're almost as out for blood as I am.

Zeke has been doing everything he can as Sheriff, but there's only so much he can do. He's talked to every florist in a sixty-mile radius, spoke to Detective Paul and his superiors at length, and spoken to Carter's probation officer. Even the well-seasoned Zeke seems to be getting a little more ragey with every day that passes.

Yesterday, the phone calls never ended. The second the phone stopped ringing, a new number was calling. All day long.

I ended up shutting her phone off and holding Charlie while she cried for hours.

This morning she insisted on having a normal day at the office, so I'm sitting in the conference room across from them that they never use. I've kind of claimed it as my own, with Olivia's permission, that is. I get to watch out for Charlie, study for my classes, or help with the kids if they need it.

Grabbing my phone, I decided to call Drew and Everett. If they can't talk me off the ledge, I'm about to cash in that "alibi and hide the body."

"Carrington. What's wrong?" Drew answers first and I tell him to hold on while I add Everett to the call.

"What's up, Hayes?" Everett has the same slightly worried tone that Drew had.

"Carter is up to his normal bullshit. Charlie is losing her damn mind, and I can't do anything about it because I can't leave her to go throttle his ass! And! And neither of you can leave to do it for me because your lives are signed away to the goddamn U.S. military." I fume at them.

"Ok. So who do we know that isn't?" Everett asks casually. It's not surprising that he isn't trying to talk me off the ledge. I think we've all hit the point that we know this needs to end.

"Well, we've got two options. Liam, if we want him dead or Lincoln, if we want his life ruined." Liam is a former Navy SEAL sniper we worked with. He's a big guy, looks like a Russian Mafia enforcer and has the attitude of one. Kept to himself mostly, but I have no doubt he could get away with murder for the right reason and paycheck. He also conveniently owes Drew a favor for saving his ass from killing some guy in a bar fight. The guy deserved it, but it would've been career ending for Liam.

"Start with Lincoln. Hayes is there to protect Charlie for now. Send him a warning that if this shit continues, he's fucked." It's not a bad plan. So far, we have only been on the defense, letting law enforcement handle it. It's time to start some offense and see what happens.

"Alright. I'll call him and see what he can do."

The next call I make is to Lincoln. He answers and I start talking before he gets a chance to say anything.

"Hey. Need another favor."

He chuckles low in the background. "Been waiting for you to take my leash off."

"Yep. Whatever you can to disrupt his life. Freeze his accounts, cut off his power, anything to let him know we aren't fucking around anymore."

"Hell yeah, brother. I've been watching him, his obsession is on another level. He tried to hack into the security cameras at your house. I locked his ass out so fast that he didn't know what happened. He's good. I'll give him that. But not better than me."

Nodding my head, I say, "I know, man. Thanks for doing all this. It's a sick fucking game for him now. He gets off on making her scared."

"You prepared to take the next step if this doesn't work out? Liam—"

"He's option B. I don't want to drag him into this unless we need to. He's either going to let it go or get pissed off and slip up somewhere."

"Alright. I'll get started tonight. I'm gonna take my time. Slow motion. Let the dominoes fall until he's on his knees."

"Appreciate ya. Send me a bill."

"Fuck *off*. You and Reynolds would do the same for me." He's right about that. The brotherhood runs thick between all of us.

Chapter Thirty-Three

Charlie

Sunday, April 12.

Hayes has been living here for over a year now and it feels right. More than right, it feels like it's the way it's supposed to have always been. We went from a long-distance relationship to having a two-year breakup to living together. It's been a whirlwind, but this last year has been everything I could have wanted and more. He fits in seamlessly with the life I created in Three Sisters.

It's been six months since the last phone call, and all things Carter have been quiet—eerily quiet. It feels like a repeat of the last time I let my guard down.

My gut is screaming at me today, for no real reason. So, I'm choosing to ignore it.

Olivia is treating Isla and me to the spa as a thank you for all the overtime we've put in the last week, and I want to enjoy every minute. No drama, no anxiety, no Carter.

Isla is our new hire as of two months ago. She's close to my age, just graduated from the community college in Bend, and has been a damn good addition to the team. She's the most organized out of the three of us, always one step ahead, and has an upbeat attitude. I swear, she's the first to get into the office and the last to leave. Olivia was a few grades above her in high school, but she knows her family well. That's why, when she came in, saying she was interested in the job, Olivia hired her on the spot.

The three of us sit next to each other, getting pedicures, completely relaxed. Soft music plays in the background, but other than that, everyone is silent.

I choose to break the silence right as I see Olivia taking a sip of her champagne. "So, Liv. Dan put out at all lately?" Champagne spews out of her mouth, all over her nail technician. Isla's eyes widen to a comical size and I grin behind my glass of champagne.

She profusely apologizes, which only makes my smile widen.

"Charlie! Warn a girl."

Laughing, I say, "Come on, it's girl time. Spill the tea."

She shrugs. "It's been a little dry in that area. He's been working overtime, covering a lot of shifts."

"Want me to kick his ass?" Isla asks as she rebraids her light brown hair.

Now it's my turn to spew champagne all over the place. Thankfully, no nail techs were sprayed this time. Isla has always been soft-spoken and reserved. I was hoping this would bring her out of her shell and I'm glad to see it has.

Olivia giggles. "Yeah, I, by all means. Just make sure while you're doing it you let him know it's because he's not 'putting out.'"

Isla nods. "Will do. So what about you, Charlie? Please tell me we can live vicariously through you and your hunk of a man."

I smirk, "Nothin' dry over here."

Olivia pretends to gag and Isla laughs with me.

"Things are good. We're still in the honeymoon phase. Making up for a lot of lost time."

"Good for you. I'd never leave my house if I were you. You either, Liv. It's a damn shame you aren't getting it all the time. Have you tried talking to him about making more of an effort?"

I grimace without meaning too. Dan can be a sore subject for Olivia.

"Sorry, too personal?"

Olivia lightly laughs but I can tell it's just to be polite. "Nah, I'm sure the entire town knows I'd like to see my husband more. There's an ebb and flow. He's busy for a while and then takes more time off. Right now, it is just an ebb."

Isla nods and says, "I get that. Well, I'll still roshambo him if you want."

I glance at Olivia, who looks as confused as I am. "Rock, paper, scissors?"

Isla's head snaps up. "Wait, that doesn't mean, like, fight?"

Between the champagne and Isla's serious tone, Olivia and I end up laughing so hard that we are doubled over.

"No, but it would be funny to see that as well. So what about you? Not dating anyone?"

She shrugs and looks away quickly. "I've been sort of seeing Jeff. But he doesn't want to label our relationship, so I try to keep it quiet."

Olivia and I both exchange worried glances.

"Jeff, as in Mayor Waltons' son?" Olivia asks.

Isla nods, looking uncomfortable. I don't know who Jeff is but based on the fact that he's not committing and Olivia's facial expression, I'm going to assume he's a dirtbag.

Olivia shakes it off and tries to dissipate the awkward

tension that is now lingering. "I heard he was back in town! He went to Yale, right? Spent some time on the East Coast?"

"Yeah, he finished law school and then his dad wanted him back for his campaign in a few years."

"That's right! I heard he had plans to run for governor."

Isla beams in response. "Yep! Jeff is really excited about it."

I watch as Olivia tries to smile, but it doesn't quite seem genuine to someone who knows her as well as I do. "Well, I hope it all works out! If not, we can make Hayes invite some of his hunky friends to town."

"Can he just do that anyway? I wouldn't mind the eye candy." Isla responds while taking another sip of her champagne.

I chuckle. "I'll ask him to start a roster."

The rest of our spa afternoon is spent the same. Laughing and sipping champagne while getting some much-needed TLC.

Chapter Thirty-Four

Hayes

"Stealing another one of my shirts?" I ask, grinning from the doorway of our bedroom as I watch Charlie change into something more comfortable. I just picked the girls up from their spa day and delivered them to their own houses. Charlie is practically glowing and more than a little tipsy.

"Shouldn't they be *our* shirts by now?" She raises an eyebrow while pulling one of my new shirts over her head.

"Like the ones that you stole from me before I left?"

A sneaky smile plays on her lips. "That was years ago. I need to start my new collection." *New collection?*

"Wait, what happened to all the others? Charlotte Amelia! Did you burn them again?"

She scoffs back, "First of all, it was one time. Second, it was Drew's sweatshirt. Third, well, I don't really have a third other than he pissed me off." Senior year, a friend was having a bonfire and Charlie showed up in barely anything. Drew was pissed, tore off his sweatshirt and forced her to put it on. The second he looked away, she tore it off and threw it on the fire.

Needless to say, we dragged her out of the party right then and there.

I shake my head but grin at her in response.

"I would never burn your stuff!" She says as she sauntered over to give me a kiss, wearing only my shirt and a pair of underwear.

"Fine, then where is it?"

She points toward our closet. "In a box, in the attic. I honestly forgot all about it until you brought it up."

My jaw drops. I hadn't wanted to bring it up before but I've been wondering what happened to everything since I got back. "For a year! It's been up there this whole time?"

She nods and shrugs. "More like two."

I flip the lights on in our closet and the one that leads to the attic. "I'm getting it and reclaiming all *my* stolen property."

She laughs from behind me as I pull the string and the door opens. "Soooo dramatic!"

After I pull the metal ladder down, I turn to see her sitting cross-legged on our bed. With a wink, I add, "You love me and you know it."

"Just get it already so we can watch a movie." She flops back on the bed in a buzzed huff.

Chuckling, I step up onto the ladder and go in search of my stuff. My head is just about to crest into the attic when a whooshing sound comes from right above it. Instincts take over. My head automatically ducks while I descend back down the steps. My right hand is already pulling my Sig out of its side holster as the sound of splintering wood comes from above.

My feet hit solid ground, and at the same time, I trained my pistol and eyes on the hole in the ceiling.

The head of an axe—my axe, to be specific—is smashed into the 2x6 wood base that supports the attic door. The very spot that my head was just at.

Grunts of rage begin to sound from above as the person tries to yank the axe out of the wood. They're just out of sight, but my SIG is already trained on where I think their chest is. The second the axe is free, I see that it's Carter standing there. He lifts it above his head once more and I fire three shots. All three hit him in the chest in quick succession.

My body stays locked; my SIG trained on where he collapsed, not moving on the stairs.

Only Charlie's loud shriek coming from the bedroom breaks the ensuing silence.

"Sunshine, call 911." I calmly instruct, my voice steady despite the adrenaline coursing through my veins.

I hear her fumbling through the bedroom and then answering the questions the dispatcher asks. Her voice sounds panicked as she gives our address. I wish I could go to her and comfort her, let her know everything is handled and that she's safe, but I'm not moving from this spot until someone trained is here to take my place. I know each shot hit accurately, but I've seen adrenaline overcome mortal wounds before.

I briefly considered going up the ladder the rest of the way, but there's no way in hell I'm offering any life-saving measures to the man who's been terrorizing Charlie. If anything, I hope the medics take their sweet time getting here and he's pronounced dead on arrival. Dark? Morbid? Unethical? Probably all of those things. But I've killed for a lot less than protecting someone I love. If I can live with those deaths, then I can certainly live with letting this man suffer the consequences of his actions.

"Hey Char, make sure you put some more clothes on."

A small laugh that sounded more like a sob sounded from our room, but based on the shuffling and drawers being thrown open, she must be listening.

Sirens sound from the driveway a few minutes later, and I hear Charlie running to answer the door.

Luke's the first one to arrive. He walks into the closet, gun in hand, and I gesture up into the attic with a head nod.

"Three shots center mass. Collapsed to the east. I haven't moved to confirm the kill yet."

Luke nods. "Any weapons?"

I glance toward the splintered wood and say, "My fucking axe." I don't know why that irritates me so much, but really? Going after my girl and then trying to kill me with my own axe? *Salt in the wound.*

"Let's wait for backup. I'll take over. Charlie needs you."

I step back, letting him step onto the ladder and aim into the attic.

I don't know Luke very well, but I trust him. He's a good lieutenant and always seems to be respectable and fair. For a man who puts the fear of God into people with just one look, he surprisingly doesn't have an ego. I know a lot of guys who let the power of being intimidating go to their heads.

Walking backwards out of the closet, I don't turn my back until I'm out of sight of the attic.

"Charlie!" I bellow as I make my way down the hallway and into the living room. The front door is open and I find her sitting with her back against the wall, huddled into herself, her phone still in hand.

My back slides down the porch wall next to her, and she rests her head on my shoulder.

"Luke's waiting for backup."

Dan's police cruiser speeds down the driveway next. Lights and sirens. Dust flying behind him.

He nods at us, gun already drawn, going into the house to help Luke.

Medics arrive next, pronouncing him dead, and I let out my first relieved breath.

It's unfortunate that shooting Carter is the way that this ended, but there's no denying the respite I felt seeing him in that body bag.

Chapter Thirty-Five

Charlie

Odessa flew in first thing the morning after everything happened. The second she found out, she was on the next flight into town. Same with Connie. Everyone I'm closest to surrounded me and Hayes the second they could. Even Everett took leave to come out for a long weekend and will be here on Friday morning.

Drew was the only one who couldn't make it because he's about to leave for a training mission. He hasn't stopped checking in, though, constantly FaceTiming or texting one of us. He's doing everything he can to convince us to move to California or back to South Carolina. For some reason, he's putting a lot of unwarranted blame on Three Sisters. I don't think it helped that Hayes threw Olivia under the bus for hiding me from Hayes at the beginning. He's had an issue with me living here since the first conversation we had but I'm not sure even this will convince me I should move back.

Of course, I'm shaken up being here but it's not the town's fault that I had someone stalking me. Everyone here has gone above and beyond to make sure we are okay. We have a never-ending supply of casseroles, desserts, and guest rooms available to sleep in. It's overwhelming to have so many people around and calling, but there's also a sense of comfort to know we have such a supportive community behind us.

I've been on a roller-coaster of emotions. Relief—that it's over. Guilt—that Hayes had to be the one to shoot him. Sadness—that anyone could be that messed up in the head. Not even two and a half years in prison could cure the sickness in his heart.

Hayes doesn't seem affected at all, only concerned about me, which has me feeling more concerned about him. He's acting like it's just another day in the office. It's easy for me to forget that he was trained to go to war—trained to be in moments like that every day. Meanwhile, I'm sitting over here, reliving every moment that felt a little off over the last few days.

Based on all the food that was up there and the burner phone that he had, they think he was hiding for at least a week in the attic. Unknowingly, he was able to breach Lincoln's advanced security software. Every time he was in the house, he would set the security footage on a loop from the previous five minutes so that he could walk around undetected. The violation and fear that come with knowing someone spied on us from so close isn't an easy feeling to shake.

The little things started to add up now that I can look back on them. I thought Hayes was just being forgetful when he didn't put the cereal box away or that I kept forgetting to shut my dresser drawers. I can't believe how many things went missing, and I was still oblivious to the danger lurking just above our heads.

Now, I only feel safe when Hayes is within arm's reach. The irrational part of me wants to never let him go, but I know that isn't healthy. We had a very long talk about us both going to therapy last night. He wasn't exactly jumping for joy, but he didn't shut down the idea either. I think he knows how much I need it and how much I need him to support me through it. At this point, I think he'd do anything I asked if it would help me feel better.

Hayes just left for the diner with the guys five minutes ago, and as much as I would like him to come back and hold me, I know that he could benefit from some time with the guys.

"I don't understand how they could have let that monster out and the parole board didn't notify anyone that he missed his last check-in." Odessa has been huffing and puffing most of the time, angry that Carter was let out of prison early. Her tough exterior has always done a good job of hiding her scared interior, but I know she's really struggling with everything that's happened.

"Trust me, I feel the same. Detective Paul is going to raise some hell for us, though. The parole officer didn't notify him about it and he's livid." Detective Paul flew out once he found out the news as well. He hopped on a plane without anyone asking, just because he felt so close to the case. He stayed for two days but left early this morning to get back to work. Seeing him was a small slice of the closure I needed to deal with the over-three-year ordeal.

Connie nods. She's been quiet since she got here. Letting us work through our emotions without any pressure. I know this has thrown her for as much of a loop as it has everyone else but it's starting to worry me that she's keeping her opinions to herself.

Odessa sits down on the couch next to me and grabs my hand. "Are you really going to stay here? In Three Sisters? It seems like a lot." She's not wrong; it is a lot. The entire situation is a lot. I don't think I can ever go back into that house again. On the other hand, though, I don't want to leave the town.

I look at Connie, hoping she will have some sage wisdom. "What do you think we should do?"

"I like this town for you two. I have since the first time I visited a few months ago. You two will be alright here if you choose to be. Find a new house and start fresh; maybe look into buying property and building something together."

My eyes go suddenly misty at that. I love it here. I love Hayes. And I love Hayes being here.

Despite Carter, I don't want to run away from this memory like I did the last one.

It only followed me here, anyway.

Chapter Thirty-Six

Hayes

Luke and Dan both sit across from me at the diner. They asked me if I'd meet them for coffee this morning, and as much as I hate leaving Charlie right now, I know I needed to. I can't hover as much as I want to, and I know she's safe with my mom and Odessa.

"How ya holding up?" Luke doesn't say very much, but when he does, it always comes out sounding a little more gruff than most.

"About as expected. You guys know how it is. We've been trained to have that on-and-off switch. Right now, I feel numb to it. Charlie's struggling pretty badly, though."

They both nod their heads in unison.

"Let us know how we can help." Dan is the most sincere guy I've ever met. He would give the shirt off his back to anyone who needed it. I've seen him working and he treats everyone in town with the same respect. Even the ones that don't deserve it.

"Thanks, Dan. I appreciate that. Right now, we're just taking it day by day."

Luke gives a small nod of understanding before changing

the subject. "You sure I can't convince you to work at the department with us? After seeing how you handled the Carter situation, you'd be a damn good fit."

"Nope. Sorry, man. That only confirmed that I needed to get out of that lifestyle. I want to be physically and emotionally present for Charlie and our future family. I don't think I can do that if I'm focused on fighting the bad guys and putting in the hours you two do." I don't mention the main reason is that killing him was too easy. Taking someone's life like that shouldn't be second nature. Don't get me wrong—I'm glad it was. It saved my life and potentially Charlie's as well. However, that doesn't mean I want to get in deeper and become so numb that I forget the gravity of the situation.

I catch Dan's shoulders sagging out of the corner of my eye and start to realize the foot I just shoved into my mouth.

When I glance at him, he looks like I just punched him in the stomach. "Can't say I blame you there. I'm fucking up left and right with Liv. Every time I try to get home early or make more of an effort, someone else needs something. It guts me how indifferent she's become to me telling her I'll be late or can't make it. We don't fight about it anymore. It's like she's so used to me bailing that she expects it now."

Luke and I both shift in our seats, trying to figure out what to say. It's clear as day to everyone how much he loves Olivia, but he continues to choose helping out everyone else over spending time with her.

Finally, I decided to take one for the team and say what we've all been thinking. "I'm gonna shoot straight with you right now. Your family should be your number one priority at all times. Work, the town—everything else has to be below them. You're going to lose Olivia if you don't change your mindset. She loves the hell out of you, but from the outside looking in, we can all tell it's wearing on her. I'm not saying you should quit your job. But you can delegate a little more."

"Sorry, friend, but I have to say I agree. You've got an incredible wife at home who would do anything for you and does. Don't fuck it up by being the martyr. End of the day, call one of the guys just starting shift to take the call. We appreciate all you do, but your family is more important."

Dan nods, staring at his half filled coffee cup. "I don't know how my dad did it all. Parenting, his career, and becoming sheriff. He's accomplished everything he ever wanted by the age of fifty, and I'm fucking it all up before the age of thirty."

"He didn't." Luke scoffs before softening his tone. "I've been your best friend for years. I was there. Growing up, it was your mom who made sure you got to practice and had dinner. Making sure Levi was doing his homework and staying out of trouble. It was always *all* your mom, *all* the time. After she died, you and Levi raised yourselves. Your dad buried himself in more work to keep himself distracted. Yeah, he was around for the big moments. But the little ones? The ones that actually matter? He wasn't there."

"Dammit. You're right. My mom was always there to make sure we didn't realize his absence. I have no doubt that is what Olivia is doing. Making sure the kids don't see my shortcomings keeping me on a pedestal in their eyes. They have no idea how much I'm failing them all because she picks up the pieces before they have a chance to fall."

"Not too late to fix that. Show up a little more. Be the partner she needs. Charlie and I are happy to help with the kids any time."

"Let us know. I'm happy to cover some shifts, too. Anything you and Liv need." Luke offers his own support before taking a sip of his coffee. The three of us clearly aren't very good at sentimental talks, but the sentiment is still there.

Dan quickly blinks away the emotion he had stirring in his eyes and tries to smile. "Appreciate you both. I'll be taking you both up on those offers. Her and the kids are the best thing that's ever happened to me. She deserves so much more from me."

"Alright, on a lighter note. What are your plans after you graduate? Live off Charlie's COO wage for as long as you can?"

My shoulders rise in a noncommittal shrug to Luke, but I chuckle. "That's plan B. Right now, I think I want to start an agency—private security and military contracting. Hoping I can get some of the guys I worked with to come on board. They're looking for a middleman to make sure they aren't getting screwed over in the fine print.

Olivia offered to let me use the empty office they have and I've been brainstorming ways to start my own business. The idea started to form when I first talked to Lincoln about helping me find Charlie. He's been taking odds-and-ends jobs, but he doesn't have a huge outreach yet. If I could pull a few more people into it, the networking would take care of itself.

Now it's just a matter of finishing my degree and reaching out to as many people as I can.

Chapter Thirty-Seven

Hayes

Wednesday, May 6.

Everyone finally left and went back to their little corners of the nation, leaving Charlie and me time to decompress. It had been a few weeks since I found Carter in the attic when Zeke called to let me know that I've been cleared of any wrongdoing and the case has been closed. I wasn't necessarily worried, considering he had been hiding in our attic with an axe, but you still never know with these things.

Charlie and I have both been going to therapy twice a week, one session together and the other apart. The culture of the Navy, especially as a SEAL, frowned upon seeking help for mental health issues. I probably never would've gone had Charlie not insisted but I'm glad she did. I've got more baggage to work through than I thought—14 years of it, to be exact—stemming all the way back to losing my dad and everything that has happened since then.

I'd be lying if I said I wasn't surprised at how hard therapy actually is. I swear she takes a deep dive into each mental wound, poking and prodding until she drains the infection. It feels like every traumatic event is festering beneath the surface, waiting for the opportunity to kill me. All because I hadn't healed them properly the first time. I'm mentally exhausted after each session, but the weight on my shoulders already feels less heavy—or maybe she's just helping me find the mental strength to carry it all.

I still feel the need to keep Charlie as close as possible, but it doesn't feel as overwhelming anymore. It doesn't hurt that I've been working in the suite across from them. She's usually within eyesight and there aren't any attics here.

I've been putting in as many hours as I can, trying to get the ball rolling on the agency. There's a lot of guys that I served with that end up floundering after they get out. I'm hoping I can bring some in, set up a support system for those that need it, and also give us all a purpose again.

Drew has offered to do what he can while staying in the Navy, even if it's only investing as a silent partner. Hopefully, I can win him over and convince him to move up here. Same with Everett, although I can't see Everett giving up flying.

Olivia pops into "my side" of the office, pulling me out of my thoughts when she sits in the chair across from me.

"How you doing, Hayes?" She laced her fingers together, setting them on the edge of the conference table.

"Gettin' better. Things have been calm and therapy seems to be helping. Still looking for property, though." We moved out of that house as soon as we could and bought a travel trailer. Neither of us could stomach looking at that attic, and it made sense since we want to buy a few acres and build a house. Charlie seems content to be back at the Cascadia RV Park, but I'm ready for something more stable.

"Did you hear that Will Johnson listed one of his properties? It's pretty close to our house."

"Yeah? Is it a decent size? How much?"

Olivia clears her throat and purses her lips. "Well, I have an idea. But you'll have to set your pride aside and hear me out."

My pride? I already don't like the sound of this. Olivia and Dan have done way too much for us already. Knowing Olivia, she'd buy a hundred acres as a birthday present.

My eyebrows draw together, but I nod for her to continue.

"I'd like to buy the property."

My head involuntarily starts shaking before she's finished. There's no way she's buying us land. I know she has more money than half of Central Oregon, but I have to draw a line somewhere.

"No. That is a very gracious offer, but—"

Interrupting my sentence, she half yells and half huffs. "You haven't even let me offer anything!"

She takes a deep breath and looks me dead in the eye. "I want to buy the property so that Dan and I can build on it, but before I do that, I want to subdivide it. You could buy a lot with however many acres you wanted."

"Oh." Feeling like a dumbass for jumping to conclusions, I apologize and ask for her to continue.

"You know I love you two and I'd love it if you were my neighbors. I've been thinking about a new house for a while now, but I haven't found one yet. This one feels right, and it's a good investment. Personally and for the business. You and Charlie could benefit as well."

I nod; she's speaking my language now. Sensible and practical. The more I think about it, the more the idea grows on me. "Let us know the details, and hopefully we can make it work." I have no doubt Charlie would be over the moon to be next door to Olivia.

She glances at her phone and smiles, her entire face lighting up. "Perfect! I already put an offer in on the property and reached out to Patrick, who does the zoning and permits. He's confident we can get everything approved quickly."

A low chuckle escapes. When it comes to efficiency, Olivia is an unparalleled expert. "You've been planning this for a while, haven't you?"

"Yep. Now I get to go claim my five bucks. I bet Charlie that I could convince you it was a good deal in under four minutes." She wiggles her fingers over her shoulder as she leaves and I realize I just got swindled.

An hour later, I'm lost in thought again, this time staring out the window down into the parking lot. A Cascadia County Sheriff SUV pulls into the parking lot and something in my gut tells me that this isn't a social visit.

I sit up in my chair, watching two deputies I've never met before get out of the SUV. The one that got out of the passenger seat walks with his shoulders and head hung so low that it sends chills down my spine. He can't stop running his hands down his face and shaking his head, surely gearing up to deliver whatever bad news he has. I've seen the look before— the day Charlie and Drew lost their parents.

My body freezes as the memories begin hitting me like tidal waves that threaten to drown me. Deputy Marco arrived at my mom's house after the car accident to inform us. He golfed with our dads occasionally, but I hadn't known him well. I watched him walk to the front door through the bay window with a combined look of devastation and defeat. He did his best to keep it together, but he couldn't get it all out with tears slipping down his face.

The two deputies nod at each other and then open the door, making their way into the office and up the stairs. My cowardly body refuses to move as I stare at the stairs, waiting for them to walk up. Every muscle feels tense to the point of pain, waiting for my fight reaction to kick in. So far, it hasn't, despite the fact that my brain is screaming that I should be moving.

I should be running to Olivia and Charlie, protecting them both from whatever they have to say, but I'm frozen in this chair. The names of loved ones that the news could be about run through my head like the end credits of a movie and I want to scream.

Just as the top of their heads crest the top stair, my eyes snap to the girls.

Olivia sees them first and a huge grin crosses her face as she greets them. Within a second, she realizes that something is wrong and I watch her smile fade.

Charlie, sensing her change in demeanor, looks up at me with concern in her eyes and then back to the deputies.

I watch through tunneled vision as Olivia's world is shattered and she collapses to the floor. The second I heard her Charlie scream, "No! No!" mixing with Olivia's sobs, my brain snapped out of the numbness that had enveloped it.

I went to them in five long strides. Charlie had her arms wrapped around an inconsolable Olivia.

I look at the deputies, only to see tears streaming down one man's face. He won't even look at me as silent sobs rake through his body.

"What happened?"

The stoic one that was driving looks at me with a raised eyebrow but doesn't say anything. Just like everyone else, his devastation was palpable in his eyes but he was the only one attempting to keep it together.

"Tell me what the fuck happened so I can help!"

He shakes his head and looks at Olivia, who lies crumpled on the floor, weeping.

Charlie's eyes close as she softly whispers through her tears, "Dan was shot. He's dead."

Epilogue

Charlie

Saturday, April 25.

My hands feel a little shaky as I try to get my hair to curl to perfection. Today's a big day, I can feel it in my soul. Not only do we get to see our new house for the first time, but I think today might be the day Hayes finally proposes. He's seemed nervous all morning, trying to play it off like he's just excited for the house but my gut is telling me there's more. That, and the fact that he hasn't taken his hand out of his pocket, continually fiddling with his tin of mints.

"Come on, Sunshine!" Hayes called out, his voice sounding deeper than normal in the quiet of the hotel room. Olivia insisted we stay at the Cascadia Ranch Resort while she put the finishing touches on our new house.

After the "incident" and then losing Dan, Hayes and I bought a piece of the property Olivia subdivided. We bought a travel trailer and had all the hookups installed while our house was being built. We've been able to watch the house be built from the ground up. Witnessing every step of the process, every nail hammered, and every wall painted.

Hayes has been a huge help with the construction, using his handyman skills to pitch in wherever he can. Olivia still wanted us to have the "wow" factor of seeing everything done for the first time, though. She hired movers, an interior designer, and a landscaping team to make sure everything was perfect for our big reveal. Even despite everything she's going through—losing Dan, being a single parent, running a business, building her own new home—she's still managed to think about the little details for us. Going above and beyond to make sure our new house felt like home from the moment we walked in.

I take one last look in the full-length mirror before walking out. My new white dress has lace lantern sleeves with an a-line silhouette and a tiered ruffled hemline. It didn't feel too short before but now that I have on a cute pair of black wedges, it's pushing some boundaries. I contemplated changing but, seeing how killer my legs look, I decided against it. I look hot, and I'm going to own it.

Hayes is scrolling on his phone, and I clear my throat to get his attention while I saunter over to where he's sitting. He does a double take when he sees me, and a slow grin spreads across his face.

I loosely hang my arms on top of his shoulders while I run my fingers through the back of his hair.

He leans back, letting his gaze roam freely as his big hands grasp the back of my legs. Lust and admiration fill those golden eyes.

"You're so fucking beautiful, Sunshine."

"Not too short?" I ask while winking, knowing he loves when I show off my legs.

"Perfect," he replies, pulling me closer for a kiss. I dodge it and turn so that he's only kissing my cheek.

"Good, but you're not smearing my lipstick. *Yet.*" I wink and step back.

Pulling up to the driveway felt like an out-of-body experience. My knees bounced as I leaned as forward as possible, trying to take in the moment and see everything. Trees line the now paved driveway and we follow them to the front of the house. Our two-story log home stands tall and welcoming, with natural stones that accent the front porch. Hanging baskets overflowing with flowers are on either side of the door, brightening up the entrance. I can't believe this is really our dream home. All of our dreams are starting to come true.

Hayes says, "One second," before getting out of his truck and making his way to my side. He opens my door and helps me out. We walk hand in hand toward the house, but before we get to the first step, he stops.

Tears begin to blur my vision before I look at him. This is the moment I've wanted since I was a little girl and developed my first crush.

His knee hits the ground and my heart soars in my chest.

He pulls the antique box out of his pocket and all I can smell is peppermint. "Charlotte Amelia Reynolds, you are the sun that my world has always revolved around. Not a day has gone by that I haven't loved you or longed for you. There is nothing I want more in this world than for you to be my wife, the mother of my children, and the one I spend the rest of my life loving. You're my best friend, my soulmate, and the owner of my heart. Will you marry me, Sunshine?"

My tears of joy turn into sobs as I nod vigorously, unable to form words through the overwhelming emotions. "This ring has been in here since before my last deployment. You didn't know it, but you still carried it around everyday that I was gone." I can barely see through all the happy tears. I knew Hayes would have a heartfelt proposal but I never expected it to be this perfect. I feel like the luckiest woman alive, standing in front of the home we built together, where every dream we've ever had is coming to fruition and new dreams will be born. This moment is everything I've ever wanted and more.

He reaches for my shaky hand with his steady one and places the ring on my finger. A beautiful cushion cut with a diamond band. It must have cost a fortune, but in that moment, all I could see was the love and commitment behind the gesture. I wouldn't have cared if he proposed with a silicone ring; the sentiment is still the same. I get to spend the rest of my life with Hayes.

Hayes wipes away my tears and whispers, "You and me, forever."

I smile while staring at the ring on my finger, placed on his hard chest. "This is the best day of my entire life."

"Mine too. Ready to see the rest of the house?" Nodding, I turn. I've lost a little bit of the steam behind seeing the inside, ready to call my family and tell them the good news, but I know that can wait. I want to live in the present and enjoy the first moment we step into our future.

"Let's do it, fiancé."

He opens the front door for me, and when I step inside, everything is perfect. The dark stained trim contrasts with the light walls and beige furniture we picked out. The great room, dining room, and kitchen are all open and connected. Hayes picked out an enormous dining room table that has a beautiful floral centerpiece. Our kitchen isn't huge, but the counters are all butcher block and the stainless steel appliances give it a modern touch.

"It's everything I wanted." Tears spill again as I hug Hayes and bury my head into his chest.

"There's one more thing I want to show you." He grabs my hand and guides me to the patio.

Through the French doors, I see more overflowing flower baskets, but the real surprise isn't what I see on the patio; it's who.

I fling open the door and throw my hand in the air, showing off my new ring. Connie, Odessa, Everett, Olivia, Ellie, and Ben shout and cheer at the same time.

Odessa is the first to hug me, followed by Connie, who whispers in my ear, "Your mom and I dreamed of this moment." An overwhelming feeling of love and gratitude hit me as I looked around at my closest friends and family celebrating with me.

Everett is face-timing with Drew, who is looking slightly teary-eyed as well, and I'm so thankful even he gets to be part of this. I held the phone and showed off my giant rock.

"It really is the perfect date." Everett's cheeky grin is in full force as he holds up a champagne glass. "April 25th, not too hot, not too cold."

Odessa rolls her eyes but holds her glass up next to his, finishing his joke. "All you need is a light jacket."

Everyone stares at them, waiting for the punchline or reference. With these two, it's guaranteed to be a rom-com.

Hayes gets it first. "Miss Congeniality? Of all the movies? You choose Miss Congeniality?"

Everett shrugs and his smile gets even wider. "You chose the date, my friend."

Odessa laughs and clinks her glass with Hayes', "Don't complain, it could've been much worse knowing Ev."

Olivia and the kids have been hanging back, smiling from a distance. I assume it's because she doesn't want to intrude, but that isn't how this family works. She should be as involved as everyone else, especially because I can guarantee she's the one who set this all up.

I hand the phone back to Everett and yell to Olivia. "Hey, Liv! Get your ass over here and congratulate me."

She laughs and carries Ellie over. Ben follows right on her heels, and a huge smile lights up his face when Hayes reaches down to him.

"Congratulations! I'm so happy for you both."

"Good, then stop being weird and come join the celebration. You're part of this family too, you know."

Olivia blushes and nods, her eyes going misty. We've been through the wringer the last few years together, both holding each other up when we needed it. I wouldn't be standing here today in my dream house, engaged to my dream guy, if it weren't for her.

"Auntie Char!" Ellie reaches for me, and I take her from Olivia.

"What do you think, Ells? Do you like my ring?"

Her eyes go wide and she grins. "'s so sparkly!"

"It is! Hayes picked out the prettiest one."

"More like the biggest one." Everett chuckles from his seat at the patio table. Connie and Odessa are already sitting next to him.

"Nothing wrong with that," I say while winking at him.

"Y'all come, eat!" Connie motions toward the table.

Everyone sits and begins to eat, drinking champagne like its water and sharing stories.

We're all still sitting on the patio when the sun begins to set over the Cascades', casting a warm glow over the pond we had designed. Hayes and I share a knowing look, our hearts are full of gratitude for the love and laughter that surround us. Despite everything bad that has come our way, we've made it through to the other side.

Also by TJ Deal

Already ready for more TJ Deal? Read on for a sneak peek of Book 2 in The Cascadia County Series—Behind the Juniper.

Chapter One
Andrew

Thump. Thump. Thump. My thumbs drum a slow, steady beat on the steering wheel, helping me calm my nerves. My girlfriend, Heather, and I have a thirty-minute drive from the airport to the small town of Three Sisters, Oregon. After seven years, my little sister Charlie is finally marrying my best friend, Hayes. I should be ecstatic, and I am, but my mind has been stuck in conflict mode since my last deployment.

It doesn't help that this rental car makes me feel like I'm driving a golf cart. It sways with every large gust of wind on the highway. My 6'3" frame is crammed into the driver seat, causing my knees to hit the steering wheel. I glance at Heather; her small frame fits perfectly in the passenger seat.

I try to focus back on the scenery before me as I drive. Sagebrush and juniper trees line the highway. The Cascade Mountains only grow larger, the closer we get to the town. My only hope is that the beautiful landscape Central Oregon has to offer can pull me out of my funk.

When the wind blows the powdery snow across the fields and the highway, I clench my teeth and grip the steering wheel harder. My eyes involuntarily begin scanning the road. Watching for the next possible threat, both in front of me and behind me. It feels like I've been on high alert for months now—if I'm being honest, years. In my career, if you're not vigilant, you're dead. That doesn't just turn off when you go on vacation, especially after the shit I just dealt with.

I've only been stateside for the last three weeks, after a grueling six months overseas. It's safe to say that I still haven't adjusted back to civilian life. At this point, I'm not sure if I will. I can't help but wonder how much more I have left to give. The training, the deployments, missing my family, losing good people—it's all starting to weigh on me.

Heather sits blissfully unaware of my unease as she chatters on about whatever mindless topic she thinks of—trying to "catch me up" on all the things I missed the last few months I was gone. Her gossip is usually mind-numbing enough to distract me, but today it only feels trivial.

I let out a heavy sigh while trying to readjust in my seat. Heather and I have felt off for a while now. We started dating in high school, nearly twelve years ago. Since then, our relationship has been a rollercoaster ride, filled with ups and downs, breakups, and fights. By the grace of God, we've managed to hold on to each other through it all and make it through to the good times. Recently, though, the good times are fewer and farther between.

Heather's hand reaches out and touches my arm, catching me off guard. I instinctively jerk away from her touch, and she recoils from my reaction.

"You good?" She asks with concern dripping from her voice, but when I glance over at her, the narrowing of her eyes feels more accusatory than sympathetic.

"Just uncomfortable; I'm not built for small cars."

"No, you definitely aren't," she giggles and winks one of those baby blues.

There it is. Our safe place—the place in our relationship where we've never struggled. Flirting and sex.

I take a second to admire her; her long platinum hair is curled to perfection, and her make-up is still flawless. She looks like she's heading to a photoshoot, not just getting off a three-hour flight that required us to be at the airport at 04:30.

I grab her hand, pulling it to my lap, and let our hands rest on my thigh while I focus back on driving.

"We should be there soon. Are you excited to see Charlie and Hayes?"

"Hell yeah," I say with a natural smile forming. It's been nearly a year since they came to visit me in San Diego.

Charlie and Hayes have been put through every test in the book and still managed to stay together. I wasn't thrilled when I originally found out Charlie left South Carolina, but as we drive through the little town she settled in, I can see the appeal. I feel like I'm finally starting to understand why Hayes didn't drag her back home to Heartsville.

Everything appears to be on Main Street, and traffic slows down as we drive by storefronts that look like they were built in the late 1800s. The street is lined with busy shops and restaurants that show off the same unique Western style. The temperature gauge reads twenty degrees on the dash and snow falls lightly, yet everyone in this town seems happy. Kids run ahead and play as their parents walk behind them, holding hands and laughing. It looks like something from a Hallmark movie, and I surprisingly don't hate it.

"Can you believe Charlie found this place?" I glanced at Heather, expecting her to have the same reaction. She's from Heartsville as well and used to talk about moving back home and starting a family. Once her career as a social media influencer took off, though, she started referring to Los Angeles as home and stopped talking about marriage and kids.

"Yeah, it's just so... Oregon Trail," she let out a small laugh.

I feel my eyebrows knit together for a second, and then it dawns on me, "The computer game we played in Mr. Smith's 7th grade class?"

"Yes! I hated that game; I always lost all my supplies in the river and then died of, like, dysentery."

Chuckling, I reassure her she has nothing to worry about: "Just leave the food and the river fording to me, and I think we will be okay."

"I will, ya big bad 'frogman.' You could probably just swim all of our stuff across those rivers, anyway."

I flexed my arm a bit and wiggled my brows at her as we turned down the winding road that leads to the resort. I've been a Navy SEAL for the last ten years and have quite the reputation going for me.

Tall pine trees line the driveway, getting thicker as they lead deeper into the forest. The trees open to reveal the resort, which looks like it was plucked out of Aspen and set down in the middle of Oregon. The Cascade Mountain Range is covered in snow and practically glows behind the three-story brick building, which resembles more of a palace than the "typical ski lodge" Charlie described.

The Cascadia Ranch Resort exudes an air of luxury and elegance with its grand entrance and meticulously maintained surroundings. This place is breathtaking, from the architecture to the groomed landscaping that still looks natural. Not a piece of litter on the ground, overgrown shrub, or single leaf out of place.

I glanced up just in time to see the valet jump out of his seat and start rushing toward our car from his booth. He isn't very far, yet my eyes track him the entire time, unease building in my stomach at his erratic movements. By the time he reaches for my door, he has a massive grin plastered on his face. It's only then that I realize I've been subconsciously feeling for my rifle the entire time, ready to neutralize the threat. Except he isn't a threat. He's practically a kid, doing his job

The guilt eats at me as I realize my fuckup. I quickly lower my hand, hoping he didn't notice my instinctive reaction, and force a smile as I exit the tiny car.

"Hello, Sir! Will you be staying with us?"

I nod, forcing myself to smile back. "Our check in isn't until later, though."

"No problem, I can take your bags and then get them to your room when it's available."

The unease from my overreaction was still with me for the rest of our conversation as I helped unload our luggage and handed over the keys. So much so that I end up giving him a more than generous, mostly guilt fueled, tip.

I take a deep breath and close my eyes, taking a second to let the woody Juniper smell that is lingering in the cold air ground me for a moment. Then I let it go and made my way over to Heather, who appeared to be having a flirty conversation with the other valet attendant.

Between my sudden approach and expressionless face, the chump starts scrambling over his feet. He's quick to apologize for any inconvenience caused, while also trying to welcome us to the resort.

I can't help but smirk as Heather steps in front of me and smacks me in the chest while rolling her eyes. She's obviously annoyed that the poor guy felt threatened merely by my presence.

Chuckling, I whisper in her ear as we enter the lobby, "I'm either inspiring or intimidating. If he chooses to be intimidated, that's on him for being weak."

She turns around and wraps her arms around my waist. "Well, maybe next time try that million-dollar smile instead of your normal 'resting bitch face,' and he may act differently."

I mock being offended with a little gasp, "'Resting bitch face?' How dare you?"

She slips out of my grasp and gently pushes me away. "Come on, you big ogre, let's go check out this bougie place."

We walk hand in hand through the lobby. The front desk is discreetly located off to one side, providing guests with a panoramic view of the mountains. The floor to ceiling windows somehow magnify the snow peaks, making it look as if you could step out into them. It's surprisingly even more spectacular inside than it was outside.

I take a second to look around before checking my phone to see where everyone is meeting. The lobby features a coffee shop, a local gift store, three fire places with couches, and an enormous bar. I could spend the entire trip right here. Just get me a blanket and a beer, and I'd be happy to pass out on one of the couches.

Scanning the group chat that Charlie set up with me and seven other people, I found the itinerary she set up. "They're meeting in the ballroom in twenty minutes. Do you mind if we just go there now and wait?"

Heather lifts one shoulder, indifferent. "Sure, I guess I can scout out some shots for my Instagram story on the way. You know, keep the 'Heathies' updated on my adventures."

I internally groan at her calling her 1.4 million followers "Heathies." Considering that 70% of them are men who want in her pants, I doubt they care where she is—only that she's half naked. Even though I'm aware that she is making an incredible amount of money, the fact that it is all based on her appearance is a bit concerning. She's one step behind OnlyFans at this point.

"Hey, this isn't a work trip, remember?" I nudge her with my elbow as I try to make light of the fact that she seems to only care about photo opportunities.

"Excuse me, but I have to work. That's how I make my living! I can't just jet off to some small, unknown town on a whim and not take advantage of the opportunity to create content for my followers. Plus, you never know, this place might have some hidden gems that could boost my engagement even more." Her dedication to her career has always been undeniable, and I used to admire her for it. Somewhere along the line, though, her content changed and now it all feels superficial.

"A whim? It's Charlie and Hayes' wedding; you've known them for over *twelve* years."

She abruptly stops walking, her overpriced white sneakers squeaking on the exceptionally clean floor as she throws her hands in the air.

I brace myself; I should have known better. She has always been one to throw an epic tantrum when someone challenges her.

"Are you *kidding* me? Charlie never even asked me to be one of her bridesmaids!" She crosses her arms, glaring at me, waiting to shoot down any rebuttal I have before she continues. I don't; I have no control over what Charlie does or doesn't do, so I just stay silent. "And Hayes? He barely even acknowledges my existence! I was only invited because I'm your date." *Here we go again.*

It's unbelievable that even after all this time, she's still fixated on his lack of interest in her. She throws it in my face whenever I bring up Hayes, who has only ever been polite toward her. I've tried to talk to him about it, but he just shrugs it off, saying she's not his girl or his problem. I get it; he's always been naturally reserved toward people he isn't close with. I can acknowledge that it may be partly my fault. Hayes has been my confidante since before we even knew what that word meant. He's always the one I go to when I need to vent during fights and inevitable break-ups. I have no doubt he's built some resentment toward her over the years, but I don't know how to fix it at this point.

She is who she is, and he is who he is.

"Look, I'm sorry you're feeling that way. I know..." I scramble for words that won't undercut her feelings or talk badly about Charlie and Hayes. "I know things have always been strained, but I really appreciate you coming with me and spending time with my family."

She uncrosses her arms and looks slightly more appeased, so I pull her into a hug. "Maybe we can get a workout in tomorrow before they need me. I can record you for some content and give you some tips you can share." That has her brightening up immediately as she begins chatting excitedly about how much Ian, her social media manager, will love that.

I try not to roll my eyes at the mention of Ian; the guy has been a pain in my ass for the last two years. Trying to convince me to be in all her stuff and promote that I'm a SEAL, ignoring the fact that it could put my career in jeopardy being that public. It's been an argument popping up more often than not, so I tend to just ignore his name.

We followed the signs down the wide corridor, toward the ballroom. The dark wood floors contrast against the warm cream walls, making each step seem more luxurious than the last. We passed at least three small alcoves that feature stone fireplaces, lounge chairs, and impeccable views. The secluded-ness they offer has me yearning to sit down and get lost in a good book.

It's not long before we see large double doors that are already open, an elegant sign that says "ballroom" is overhead.

Even I feel impressed with how incredible this room is. The front of the room features an imperial staircase that leads to an upstairs balcony. Beyond the staircase, the ballroom appears to be fully set up for the reception tomorrow.

Tucked between the dance floor and expansive floor-to-ceiling windows are opulent couches that overlook a meadow right below the mountains. A full bar and tall tables sit off to the right, and to the left is a long table set up for the reception dinner. The decorations appear to only be floral arrangements of all different colors, sizes, and heights. The atmosphere is fun and elegant, just like Charlie.

My admiration grinds to a halt when I spot a woman behind the long table, teetering atop a ladder, rifling through the bouquets.

She's wearing a long-sleeve fleece button-up flannel, short black running shorts, and dusty cowboy boots. Her brown hair is thrown into a tight pony that swishes behind her as she moves.

My jaw drops when she yanks another flower out of the bouquet, muttering something under her breath, and tosses it carelessly down below her. It feels like my brain is struggling to comprehend who this lady is and why she's dismantling Charlie's centerpieces at a five-star resort.

Heather notices where my gaze has landed and immediately stalks over to the woman.

"Excuse me," she says, starting to scold the woman.

When it's clear she still hasn't noticed us yet, Heather glances over her shoulder at me like, "What the fuck is happening?"

I shrug and motion for her to continue.

"Hello! What are you doing?" she yells, placing both hands on her hips.

The woman startles and quickly turns to look at us, nearly

falling off the ladder. "Oh, shit!" She grabs onto the ladder, catching herself. "Sorry." She holds on this time and looks up at us, her smile getting brighter when she seems to recognize us. "Oh, hey! You must be Drew and Heather! I knew your flight was early, but you guys made great time!"

I bristle at her familiarity. Who the hell is this woman? Hardly anyone calls me Drew; it's either Andrew or Reynolds, mainly depending on whether I'm in uniform or not.

"It's Andrew," I corrected her, my tone clipped. "Who are you?"

Her smile falters for a moment, taking in my hostility. "Oh, I'm Olivia, Charlie's friend and... boss?" She scans my face while talking, noticing the lack of interest, and then adds the last part like it's a question. Her left hand reaches over to twirl her wedding ring, the tell-tale sign of her nervousness.

I recognize her name immediately, and my mood only grows more sour.

Hayes briefly mentioned her when he was looking for Charlie in Three Sisters, a few years ago. All that I really know about her is that she's married with kids, Charlie started working for her, and then she lied to Hayes when he called to talk to Charlie. Since then, I tend to tune out any mention of her.

"Great." My voice drips with sarcasm. "What the fuck are you doing?"

When she notices my temperament toward her hasn't changed, her expression morphs from apprehension into defiance. She plucks another flower—a white rose—and narrows her eyes at me.

"Your sister despises roses—well, white roses," she twirls the flower pointedly, "but especially white ones." She looks at me, one eyebrow raised and lips slightly pursed. "The whole stalker, harassing her situation." She drops the flower like it's a mic drop, effectively putting me in my place. I flinch as remorse and anger surge through my body; it happens every time I think about Charlie's stalker.

Charlie left South Carolina because of a neighbor who fell in love with her and began stalking her. The man went from friendly to obsessive when Charlie didn't return his interest, doing everything he could to get Charlie's attention. Feeling backed into a corner, she just left. She wouldn't tell anyone where she was or where she was going. Charlie was practically a ghost; aside from the occasional contact she had with Hayes' mother, Connie, she was nearly untraceable.

It took Hayes close to a month to track her down and discover what was going on. He even gave up his career as a Navy SEAL to be with her. He found her here, put an end to the stalker situation, and won her back in the process. I respect the hell out of him for giving it all up and protecting her like that.

Olivia continues on her rant. "The florist must have forgotten, even though Charlie *repeatedly* told her she didn't want them," she adds, emphasizing her annoyance with the florist. Her tone becomes somber as she sighs, "I'm just trying to fix the mistake before she gets here." Her brown eyes almost look a little misty-eyed, but she quickly blinks them away and gets back to work on the bouquet.

I may have my issues with Olivia for playing a role in hiding Charlie from us, but I can at least acknowledge her loyalty to my sister. I pinch the bridge of my nose, nodding my sentiments.

Heather, on the other hand, decides to ignore the good deed Olivia is doing and hits her with a jab instead. Distain drips from her voice as she motions toward Olivia's boots and shorts, "And the outfit? To a 5-star resort?"

I almost chuckle; she isn't wrong. Olivia looks like she couldn't decide between going to the gym or a rodeo.

When Olivia looks down at her outfit, her eyes widen slightly, and then she lets out a loud, vibrant laugh. "Isla, Charlie's assistant, called me in a panic when she saw the florist bringing the flowers. I guess when I raced out the door, I instinctively just put on the closest shoes I could find."

Who instinctively puts on shit kickers that look like they truly only kick shit?

Charlie and Hayes chose that moment to walk through the door. Hayes noticed me first, giving me a chin tip as a broad grin crossed his obnoxious face. "'Bout damn time your ugly mug showed up," he bellows through the room.

Charlie looks over, her expression making all the drama this morning worth it. "DREW!" she beams as she sprints to me.

I lift her up and spin her around before setting her down. "Hello, Mrs-soon-to-be-Carrington!"

The scoff in the background comes straight from Olivia.

Hayes nods and says hello to Heather, but bypasses her as he walks over to Olivia. Indirectly proving Heather's point that he doesn't care for her. I watch him whisper to Olivia, but I can't make out what they're saying.

I glance back to Charlie, who is chatting animatedly with Heather, giving me the opportunity to step a little closer to Olivia and Hayes.

In a hushed voice, he lets out a string of curse words, followed by, "I owe you, Liv. Thanks."

She smiles and gestures with her head toward Charlie, "All good. Just get her out of here before she decides to call the florist and raise hell."

He rubs the back of his neck and nods. "Maybe she deserves a good ass chewing, though."

"Don't worry, I already handled it. The florist is giving you a small refund and waving the delivery fee."

"You're the best. I'll distract her; we were planning on showing the new arrivals around town anyway."

Her smile dims a bit at the mention of Heather and me. She glances at us, but quickly looks back to Hayes when she catches me staring. The sugary smile is back as she tries to hide her mixed feelings toward us. "Great, have fun!"

With that, Hayes starts hustling us out of the room, ignoring Charlie's protests that she didn't get to talk to Olivia. Putting my arm around her, I poked at her rib. "Let's go, little Sis! Show me this town you can't bear to leave."

About the Author

TJ Deal is a Pacific Northwest-based aspiring author who often daydreams about writing stories in the incredible places she travels to around the world. Thanks to her husband's unwavering support and her lifelong obsession with reading, she has decided to follow her passion for writing. Her days are mostly spent drinking coffee, relishing in the daily grind of motherhood, and capitalizing on every free moment to work on her latest novel.

instagram.com/Tjdealauthor

amazon.com/stores/TJ-Deal/author/B0D42FS93Q?ref=sr_nt-t_srch_lnk_2&qid=1717628245&sr=1-2&isDramIntegrated=true&shoppingPortalEnabled=true

tiktok.com/@tjdealauthor

Also by TJ Deal

Behind the Cascades

Behind the Juniper

Behind the Larch